THE SIX THINGS
WE SHARE

Otto Frank Miller

Big Water Press

LAKE OF THE OZARKS, MISSOURI

Otto Frank Miller/Big Water Press
Lake of the Ozarks, MO 65020
www.bigwaterpress.com

Book Editing by Laura Popelka

Cover Design by Renee Robbins
©reneerobbins.com 2021. All rights reserved.

Publisher's Note: This is a work of fiction. Names, characters, places, and inci-dents are a product of the author's imagination. Locales and public names are sometimes used for atmospheric purposes. Any resemblance to actual people, living or dead, or to businesses, companies, events, institutions, or locales is completely coincidental.

The Six Things We Share/ Otto Frank Miller. -- 1st ed.
ISBN 978-1-7364200-0-3

For Sofia and Julia

CONTENTS

1

CAROLES AND DARYLLS

"This ain't my business and I ain't making it my business," she said.

"Sorry, sister, it's your business now." Janet closed the bedroom door, trapping them both inside.

The woman swallowed hard and fidgeted with her hands.

"Don't worry," Janet continued, "I still need a roommate and your background check came back perfect."

"You actually think I'd stay in here?" The woman pointed to where the bed had been before it was reduced to splinters.

"You were supposed to move in tomorrow."

"I know, but you already gave me the key," the woman explained. "I thought I'd drop some boxes off,"

"What's your name again?" Janet asked.

"Ashley. Ashley Pemberton." She lowered her forehead and peered at Janet. "We just had coffee yesterday. That's when you gave me the key, remember?"

"I'm going to call you Carole."

"Hey, listen Janet, you've clearly got some stuff to deal with here." Ashley moved toward the door.

Janet blocked her way. "Will I see you? Are you going to come back?"

Ashley fidgeted with her hands again. She looked down and that's when she noticed the mallet. It was resting on its head, hidden from view until Janet had stepped in front of her.

Ashely summoned her gumption and stuck out her chin. "No, I don't believe I will. I'd like to leave now."

"I'm keeping your security deposit; your first and last month's rent, too." Janet cocked her head, wondering if the new fact set would sway the woman.

Ashley stared silently, perhaps contemplating her account balances. "Why are you doing this to me?"

Janet told her sweetly, "Because you came early."

"What happened here?" Ashley pointed to the busted furniture.

"I thought you said you didn't want to make it your business, Carole?"

"My name is Ashley."

"I like Carole."

"What happened to your old roommate? Is she all right?"

"She's fine," Janet said and shrugged. She reached down and grabbed the mallet's handle.

Ashley took a step back. Janet took a step forward. The mallet swung low. The business end swept back and forth like a pendulum.

Ashley whimpered. Her hands began to tremble and the spasms spread up her arms to her shoulders. She put her hands to her mouth and shuddered between short, quick breaths. "I'll come back tomorrow, I promise."

"I know you'll be here tomorrow, Carole, I just know it." Janet let the swinging mallet's momentum carry itself up to her waist. The mallet head landed in her left palm.

Thud

Ashley stepped backward and stumbled on a broken piece of headboard. She assessed the window as she looked over her shoulder to catch herself. The apartment was on the third floor.

"Please, you can keep the money, no matter what," Ashley bargained.

"I don't want money. I want a roommate."

"What the fuck is wrong with you?!" Ashley screamed and broke for the door.

Janet didn't budge. The door swung open before Ashley and there was another woman standing there with a mallet raised. She was dressed exactly like Janet. Her mallet matched as well.

The woman smashed the eight-pound load of cast iron into the crown of Ashley's skull. Ashley's form spilled into a pile at the threshold.

"Hello, Carole," Janet greeted the bludgeoner.

"Hello, love," she replied.

"Is there room in the trunk?" Janet set her mallet on the dresser carefully and caressed the handle with her index finger before turning to Carole.

"Yes, love. I'll put this Carole with that Carole."

"The New Year's show is postponed," Craig told Kayla.

"You can't postpone the new year," Kayla answered dryly.

"Says here 'Nora Lynn Donovan's New Year's show in Austin postponed'."

"OK, that makes more sense," Kayla said. "Do they say why?"

"It just says it's postponed."

"Until when?"

"Doesn't say."

"Will there be refunds?"

"Doesn't say."

"Let me see." Kayla reached her hand around Craig's laptop and turned it toward herself.

Craig stood from his kitchen counter stool and wheeled the laptop back toward himself. He shut it and set it aside. "Why do you have to see everything for yourself? Why can't you just trust me?"

Kayla grabbed her empty coffee cup and walked to the sink. She rinsed it out, squeezed a drop of cleanser in the bottom and washed it. She set the cup rim-side down in the drying rack and turned. "I know you don't want to go down there."

"Why do you keep obsessing?" Craig met his palms, as though to pray. "I bought the plane tickets. I booked the hotel. I bought the concert tickets. Are these the actions of someone who doesn't want to go?"

"You're looking for a reason to back out. That's why you said New Year's was cancelled."

"I said the SHOW was cancelled. Not the holiday." Craig spread his arms and bent forward at the waist. "You have to stop with this. Your lack of confidence is very unbecoming."

"Unbecoming of what?"

Craig tried to walk it back. "I mean, I shouldn't have to keep proving that I want to be with you, that I'm devoted to you."

"Why did she write you again?" She asked, pointing to his laptop.

"Oh my God. You've got to stop."

"I saw it. I saw it when I looked at your computer. She wrote you again." Kayla thrusted her index finger at the computer. "It was new. It was unread."

"If it was unread, how the hell would I know what it said?" Craig yelled.

Kayla stared back at Craig, unmoved by his airtight logic.

"Fine, here." Craig turned the laptop for her to see.

Suddenly aware of her childishness, Kayla shrunk with shame. Still, she couldn't resist the opportunity. She leaned in and the monitor's glow reflected on her face. "Says here you're eligible for a hair-loss study at Griffon University."

Craig combed his fingers through his thick, dark hair. "Well, maybe I could be part of the control group." He smirked.

Kayla smiled but then quickly looked back to the monitor. She opened the message and read it aloud.

Thank you, Craig. You're right. I think I knew that all along, but I needed to hear it from someone I trust. I appreciate you. You're a good consigliere!

Best,
Janet

Kayla looked at Craig, puzzled. She turned the laptop back toward him. He peered down, read and turned the laptop back toward Kayla. "Read the rest of the messages." He pointed at the monitor.

Kayla scrolled to the very bottom of the thread. She sped through the prior two messages.

Carole and I are on the rocks again . . . she was way too drunk and said a lot of hurtful things . . . I love her but I can't handle her temper . . . every decision carries so much more gravity now that we live together, you know? I need some good advice . . . I'm worried that if I'm too rash, I'm going to regret the consequences.

"Oh my." Kayla raised her brow.

"Did you read my reply?"

Kayla's face darted back to the monitor. She scrolled to Craig's response.

. . . There is no such thing as passion without emotion. Carole gives you that passion you desire, but you have to accept everything that comes with that. She will be angry, she will make you angry, but you will bring each other joy too. Sometimes – like now – you will be sad, and you will struggle. The choice is whether to sacrifice your short-term happiness for long-term good. It's up to you to decide if that's a good trade. And it's normal to be afraid of what happens if you guess wrong. All I can say is that if you take the risk, she just might surprise you with a bigger payoff than you ever imagined . . . .

Kayla slammed the monitor down. "You disgust me."

"What?"

"You disgust me." Kayla smiled. "You're too damn sweet and helpful."

"Take it easy, would you please?" Craig sipped his coffee. "I haven't even finished this yet."

She hugged him, then she rested her head on his chest. The fuzz on his sweater irritated her cheek so she pulled back and looked up at him. "I love you."

"I suppose you do." Craig smirked. "Can I ask you a question?"

"Anything."

"Why did I pay for a garage slip for you if you aren't going to use it?" Craig peered over Kayla's head to the alley that ran behind the row of townhomes. Kayla had parked her car outside.

"I thought I was running back out last night. Sorry." She began collecting her things to head to work.

"It's freezing outside."

"I know, that's why I got this." Kayla raised her key fob and pressed a button. The engine on her sedan roared to life outside.

Craig raised his hand, holding a fob as well. He pressed the button and another engine roared to life in front of the home.

"What's your excuse?" Kayla asked.

"It wasn't this cold when I came home last night," Craig said as he slipped the laptop into his courier bag.

"Hey, why didn't you tell me Janet was gay?"

"Honestly, I didn't know until she started working at GPM." Craig took his coat off the back of a chair. "I mean, she wasn't gay at one point," he added with a macho flourish that he immediately regretted.

Kayla glared.

"We were in college!" He reminded her, again. "Clearly, I didn't make much of an impression."

"Not funny."

"She's a lesbian now!" He kept on. "What's that tell you?"

"Seriously, why didn't you just tell me that instead of letting me torture you?"

"She said it was a secret. She didn't want anyone to know, especially at work."

"I don't work there," Kayla said.

"Yeah, but your best friend does," he said. "Trust me, it's easier this way. Or, was easier."

"Gay or not, I really wish she hadn't started working there."

"I hadn't seen her for eight years, and I can't control who the company hires, Kay."

"I don't want to share you, any part of you, not even your advice."

Craig sighed. "I have to go to work now."

"Have a good day. I love you."

"I love you too." Craig kissed her forehead. "Remember that we have the company holiday party on Thursday night."

The GPM holiday party was held at Sunup that year. It was GPM policy to refer to the party as the "holiday" party and not the Christmas party. Bill Tripp, head of Human Resources, was sure to enforce the religious diversity directive by way of memo, statement and—especially—through personal action.

"Merry Christmas, Bill!" An employee raised a rocks glass to Bill.

"Happy Holidays to you, Eric," Bill replied as he walked by.

"Joyeux Noel, Bill," another person said.

"Huh?"

"That's French for Merry Christmas."

This one put Bill Tripp off balance. The foreign language presented a cultural diversity moment and he didn't want to be insensitive.

"Joyeux Noel," Bill responded, prioritizing the cultural diversity directive over the religious diversity directive. As he moved on, the employee pumped her fist in victory.

Kayla bounced with anticipation as Bill drew closer to her and Craig.

"Don't do it," Craig said.

"It's a tradition," Kayla replied without taking her eyes off Bill Tripp.

"You'll never top last year."

"Challenge accepted," she said.

Bill approached. It was Craig and Kayla's turn to receive him.

"Happy holidays, Bill."

"Mr. Forsythe! Always a pleasure. Happy holidays to you, too."

"Mr. Tripp, you remember my companion, Kayla," Craig said.

"Of course. Happy holidays, Kayla."

"Thank you, Mr. Tripp. This is a wonderful party," Kayla beamed. "What a wonderful celebration of the birth of our lord and savior, Jesus H. Christ."

Bill Tripp was unfazed. "It is a celebration of all manner of things, not the beliefs of any of one group. Let's be sure to reflect on that."

"Of course, of course, but you must concede that Jesus is the reason for the season, as they say." Kayla bounced and giggled. She winked at Bill Tripp.

Bill Tripp smiled. "Happy holidays." He waved politely to Craig and Kayla and moved down the line.

Craig leaned close to Kayla, "Jesus H. Christ?"

"Yes, I felt it was appropriate for a professional function such as this."

"What does the H stand for?"

"Henry, I believe."

The room was resplendent with ice sculptures and bulbous silver ornaments the size of globes. The black surfaces of the buffet tables were so polished that they reflected the white holiday lights that hung from sconce to sconce along the walls.

Sunup was a Pan-Asian seafood restaurant in the heart of the Kubbard, the trendiest strip of clubs and restaurants downtown. There were three-tiered towers of shellfish set as the centerpiece of each table. At the base were lobster tails and crab legs, one level above were oysters and clams, and the top tier held a ring of shrimp hung tail down like hooks on the rim of a cup. On the left half of the tables there were sushi and sashimi laid out in the pattern of the yin and the yang. The seaweed sheath of the sushi provided the dark, yin component and the nude sashimi comprised the yang.

The guests ate and listened to the owner of the company boast of their successes for the year and challenges for the year to come, which they were sure to handle with aplomb. Top achievements were highlighted, awards were given, work anniversaries were noted, and several employees received fine watches in recognition of lengthy dedication.

"One last thing before I let you folks return to partying," said the owner. He took a long sip of his cocktail and then massaged his throat. "As is tradition, you will each receive your holiday bonus tonight—your bonus, bonus. As a reminder, this is in addition to your performance bonus that you will receive in February. As a further reminder, this bonus is based solely on your time employed here at GPM."

Mark from accounting had just received a watch in recognition of his twenty-five years with GPM. He waved his wrist and grinned with satisfaction.

"Yes, yes, Mark." The owner nodded and smiled. "Big night for you."

The crowd laughed and whooped.

"Bill Tripp will be around with Anita to distribute the envelopes. Please keep an eye out for him." The owner pointed to Bill and Anita standing to his right. "And with that, I wish you the happiest of holidays. Have fun tonight, be safe and if you're late tomorrow, Mark is fired."

The crowd laughed and applauded. The lights went down and the music came up. Folks queued up for drinks at the nearest bars.

"Hey, check this out." Craig pulled Kayla from a conversation she was having with one of the guests.

Craig discreetly handed his bonus envelope to Kayla. He gestured downward with his hand, signaling to her to play it cool. "Open it but not all the way. Just peak in there."

Kayla looked around, mocking his caution. She flicked the edge of the envelope with her finger, blew into the opening and stole a quick glance. She handed it back to Craig.

"So what?" she asked.

"So what? That's three thousand bucks is what," Craig said a little too loudly, catching himself and looking around.

"And that's terrific, but shouldn't your regular bonus be a lot more than that?"

"Well yeah, I hope so, but last year this one was less than one thousand," he said. "How did it more than triple in just one year?"

Kayla shrugged. "If it's a mistake, you should let Bill know. It would be foolish to risk your regular bonus for this." She flicked the envelope with her finger again.

"That's why I love you, Kay, prudent and sexy."

"SEXY and prudent," she corrected him.

"Of course, sorry."

As Craig bolted away to find Bill Tripp, Kayla caught sight of Janet. She walked over to talk to her.

"Hey, Jan," Kayla said as she drew near. They shared a half-hug and pat on the back.

"How are you, Kay?" Janet had a sweet, round face. Her dark hair was shorn in a tight, pixie style.

"I'm having a blast," Kayla gushed and raised her glass, tipping it to and fro. "Did you come alone?"

Janet hesitated just long enough to make things awkward but not unfriendly. "Nope, no date tonight I'm afraid." She waved her hand around in the air. "These folks don't know me well enough yet, if you know what I mean."

A long beat passed before Kayla answered, "Nope, don't know what you mean."

"Say, where's that hunky guy you stole from me?" Janet joked. "I assume you're here with him and not someone else?"

Kayla laughed. "I came with Bill Tripp. He just ran off, though. We're not seeing eye to eye on the whole celebration of baby Jesus thing."

"I see. Funny." Janet began to walk away, but stopped. She looked back and said, "Happy holidays, Kayla."

"Janet, wait." Kayla reached out.

Janet turned back.

Kayla took a step closer to her. "Would you like to come over for dinner sometime soon?"

Janet's brow popped. "Sure, OK. When?"

"How about Saturday night?"

Janet's mouth went crooked with a sideways grin. "I think I'm free. I'll let Craig know at work tomorrow, is that OK?"

"Sounds good." Kayla raised her glass and winked at Janet. "Bring a date."

"Jesus, you're a lightweight," Craig said to Kayla in the back of the cab.

"Cheap date!" Kayla exclaimed. She drew closer to him and kissed his neck. Craig looked up at the rear-view mirror framing the driver's eyes. He pushed her away.

"I love you, baby, but hold your horses." Craig laughed.

Kayla pumped her arms to mimic a cheerleader. She chanted, "Lightweight, cheap date, time for us to fornicate."

Craig laughed harder and they shared a long kiss. He pulled away when he felt the driver watching them again. "Hey, I solved the riddle of the bonus, bonus."

"The bonus, bonus, bonus, as it were," she corrected him.

"Bill Tripp says my holiday bonus includes a new-hire bonus; a finder's fee for bringing them a valued new employee."

"Janet?" Kayla peeled away from Craig. She moved so far back that she leaned against the door behind her.

"I know, right?" Craig said. "I never even knew she had in- terviewed until I saw her on her first day."

Kayla processed the information through her liquor-addled mind. "Are you going to keep it?"

"I mean, yeah, I guess. Bill Tripp said she put my name down as having referred her, so it's legit." Craig shrugged.

"OK." Kayla shrugged and drew back closer to Craig.

"We're going to have to find a way to thank her."

"Oh, I think I got you covered there."

"How's that?"

"I invited Janet over for dinner on Saturday night," Kayla shrunk as she said so. "With a plus one, too."

It was Craig's turn to escape to the lateral retreat of the backseat. "Why?"

"You know, there's so little time for making new friends. We started talking and I thought about what a shame it was to throw away old friendships."

"You were drunk and feeling all lovey-dovey." Craig pointed. "You're going to wake up tomorrow and regret this."

Kayla reached over and pulled at his arm, but he yanked it away.

"This is typical female bullshit. On Monday you're super jealous and can't stand me talking to her. By Thursday night, you're inviting her over for dinner." He shook his head.

"Aren't you happy that it's water under the bridge?"

"Oh, you just want to know what she's like now. You're being nosey." Craig shook his head more.

"Well, I didn't know she was, like, into the lap flounder. Did you?"

Craig tried to suppress a smile but surrendered. "No, that came as a surprise to me, too."

Friday morning at the GPM offices was like the march of the zombies. Officers hunched over their desks behind closed doors. Employees waited silently for their turn at the coffee machine. Everyone carried bottles of water. Craig used his shoulder to push through the glass doors. He carried a greasy bag of fast-food breakfast in one hand and a coffee in the other.

When he arrived at his bullpen, he saw that his three team-mates had arrived before him. Kevin waved from his seat, frowned and returned to his duties. Tom and Alex were chatting quietly in the corner. They noticed Craig and waved him over. Craig dropped a hash brown and an egg sandwich on Kevin's desk, but he pushed it away.

"How we feeling?" Craig handed them their breakfasts.

"We closed Beaumont's; got home around four," Tom told him.

"Yikes," Craig replied.

"That's nothing," Alex added. "Three guys from IT came straight in. They were out all night."

"Are they a mess?"

Alex and Tom looked at Craig like he was a fool.

"What places are open all night on Thursday?" Craig asked.

"Maybe something out by the airport?" Alex pondered. "I don't know."

Bill Tripp entered the area. He was marching down the aisle to the COO's office. Anita trailed a few steps behind.

Craig hooked Anita after Bill Tripp passed. "What's going on?"

Anita was anxious to catch up with her boss. "Can't tell you now, but someone didn't make it home to the missus last night." She scurried away.

Craig's team reunited.

"Goldfinch?" Craig guessed.

"Nah, I saw him leave early," Alex answered.

"Harrison?"

"He was with Goldfinch." Alex shook his head.

"Harold from Operations? He's been sweet on Vanessa for a loooong time," Tom speculated.

"It was Josh," Kevin spoke up.

"Josh Bogden?" Craig asked.

"Yeah."

"How do you know?" Tom asked.

"I was with him," Kevin answered.

"But you're here." Alex said.

"Am I Alex? Am I really?" Kevin put his face in his hands and breathed deeply.

GPM Holiday Party Rule #1: Always show up to work the day after the party. There was no penalty for being a little late, or looking a mess, or puking in the bathroom—but you had to show up. To not show up was to dishonor your team and yourself. And to not show up at home and have your wife calling to track you down was an embarrassment to the company and a potential legal liability.

"What happened?" Craig asked.

"He was pretty lit, but he was still standing," Kevin said without raising his head from his hands. "We went to Country Club after the party and he had a few more, and then he split."

"So, did he, like, hook up or something?" Craig asked.

"He got in a cab by himself," Kevin said. "That's the last we saw him."

"So how do you know he's the guy who never made it home?" Craig asked.

"Because his wife called me, looking for him," Kevin said.

Bill Tripp marched out of the COO's office with Anita in tow. But as Bill Tripp sped ahead, Anita slowed and circled back to Craig.

"Josh Bogden woke up in the ER," Anita whispered. "He's fine, mostly. He passed out in the back of a cab and the guy didn't know where else to take him."

"What was wrong with home?" Craig asked.

"Cabbie left his phone number at the ER. We called him and he said he took Josh to the address he gave him. We checked and it wasn't Josh's home address. Josh went in but came right out immediately, the cabbie said. Josh asked him to take him back to the bar but it was closed when he got there, and Josh was passed out anyway," she said.

"Who's house did he try to go to?"

"I can't tell you. I have to go." Anita scurried away again.

Craig didn't find time to look for Janet until after lunch. Janet was in a foul mood, but so was everyone else by the afternoon.

"Heard we'll be hosting you tomorrow night," Craig said.

"Guess so." She did not turn to acknowledge him.

"Listen, Kay was drunk, it's no big deal if . . ."

"Oh, so it was just Kayla being drunk?"

"Well, we were all a little served," Craig pled. "I mean, not as bad as Josh Bogden."

"What's that supposed to mean?" Janet shot back.

"Nothing. Nothing." Craig waved it off. "In any case, I would like you to come by so I can thank you. I never knew you put my name down as referring you."

Janet finally looked at Craig. "It felt like a waste to not take advantage of it. I knew you worked here, even if we hadn't talked in years."

Craig cocked his head. "You acted kind of surprised when I saw you on your first day."

"YOU acted surprised." She pointed. "I just went along with it."

"Yeah, I guess."

"Craig, dinner tomorrow night is fine. I'm just a little disappointed that you told her."

"We have a pretty transparent relationship, Jan."

"Well, I don't," she said. "And if Kayla just wants to gawk at me and my dyke girlfriend, I'd rather pass."

"It's not like that. We go back a long time; the three of us do."

Janet made a half smile and nodded, "Technically, I introduced you two."

Craig wagged a finger. "Nah, you thought she was getting
too sweet with your fiancé, so you nudged her my way."

"I should have let her have him," she sneered.

"Come on, how could you have ever known?" Craig put his
hand on hers. "That was a long time ago. We were still kids."

Janet slipped her hand from beneath his. She turned back to
her work. "I know, you just never know how things will turn
out, right? You were still single, and I was engaged. Look at us
now."

Craig stood. "OK, so I will see you guys tomorrow night? 6
pm?"

"Sure, shoot me a message with your address. I'll bring
wine."

Craig walked away. Janet muttered to herself, "I should have
let her have him."

Craig shut off the vacuum and wrapped the cord. Kayla in-
spected the wine glasses for smudges. She addressed
imperfections with a soft towel.

"Breaking out the nice ones, huh?" Craig asked.

"We're nearly thirty, honey, time to start acting like we have
some class."

"Why is it so important to impress her?" Craig took the tablecloth from the cabinet.

"It's not. I just want her to feel welcome."

"My mother was here for three days and we ordered in every
night."

"And?"

"Bad example." Craig grabbed the tablecloth by two corners
and unfurled it with a snap of his wrists.

Whoosh

Kayla set a glass down and joined Craig to set the table. He stopped and stared at her.

"Seriously, what's your angle?"

She stared back and dropped her voice, "It's a woman thing. Women's intuition. You won't understand."

"Are you fucking serious right now?"

"Would you relax?" Kayla concentrated on placing utensils.

"I'm relaxed. It's just that in thirty minutes, I'll be hosting my coworker slash ex-girlfriend and her new girlfriend for dinner in my home," Craig said.

"You said you wanted to repay her. What's the big deal?"

"Yes, I did, but you invited them to our home after busting my balls about her reaching out to me."

Kayla stopped setting the table and looked at Craig. "I want her to come here and see a perfect home. I want her to see a perfect relationship. A perfect, unassailable relationship so resilient that only a fool would to try to shake us."

Craig let out a sigh. "But that is what we are," he said and wrapped Kayla in his arms.

"I know. I know. And now she'll see that." Kayla wiggled away, returning her attention to the table.

Craig and Kayla finished in the kitchen. With everything in perfect order, they used their free time to put the perfectly ordered home into even more perfect order. The doorbell rang.

Ding dong

Kayla broke for the door before Craig could flinch.

"Hiiiii," Kayla sang as she opened the door to Janet and her companion. "Welcome, come in."

"Hi there." Craig waved from behind Kayla.

The guests crossed the threshold and began to remove their shoes.

"Leave them on, leave them on," Kayla told them and reached out for their coats.

Janet slipped off her coat. Beneath it she wore a tight tunic over jeans. It was emerald green with what looked like black scales on the sleeves. The jeans were tight and designer made, a perfect hybrid of cocktail and casual dress.

Janet presented her companion, "Craig, Kayla, this is Carole."

Carole looked like Janet: white skin with dark short hair framing a cherub face. She wore jeans and a tight, ruby colored top.

"Pleasure to meet you," Kayla said and reached her hand out to Carole. Carole took her hand, drew her close and placed kisses on each of Kayla's cheeks, European style.

"Thank you so much for the invitation," Carole bounced and bubbled. "Your home is beautiful."

Kayla stood still, stunned by the kisses.

"Thank you, Carole," Craig nodded and then received his kisses from Carole.

Carole reached down into the bag by her feet and pulled out two bottles of wine. "We brought wine."

"One red and one white," Janet added. "Since we didn't know what you're into."

Kayla smirked. "Good call. One never knows these days."

Dinner was grilled lamb. It was the only dish that Craig knew how to make well, a recipe passed down to him by his maternal grandfather from Greece. As a complement, Kayla added a savory pastry of filo dough filled with spinach and feta. There was a cucumber salad as a side.

Carole dominated the conversation, and Craig, Kayla and Janet seemed fine with ceding the MC duties to the newcomer.

"We need alcohol to revert to our true selves," Carole asserted as she spilled the last of the third bottle of wine into her glass. The two bottles the guests had brought were finished before the second course. "You see, we spend too much time in our professional settings, where we have to act so polite. Sadly, we begin to forget ourselves, our true selves."

"I saw some people at the work party the other night who'd be better off not being so genuine," Craig chuckled as he looked at Janet. Kayla retrieved another bottle of red and began opening it.

"Take Janet. She's a very impulsive person," Carole continued. "She'll scold me for being too loud or too forward, but you always know what you're getting with me, you know? Now Janet, on the other hand, she'll surprise you. Just add liquor and you never know who'll be knocking on your door at 3 am."

"Carole?" Janet's eyes shot daggers at her companion.

"I know . . . I'm sorry. I'm just saying you're impulsive. You get engaged, get unengaged, quit your job, leave the country, you know?" Carole's eyes sparkled as she gazed at Janet. "It's wonderful. It's exciting. I admire you."

"How about you give your voice a rest for a little bit, Care?" Janet patted her on the back.

"You're right." Carole nodded. "Kayla, tell me about how you met Craig."

"Ha." Kayla put her hand to her mouth to catch her laugh. She sat back and smiled at Craig, then answered, "Well, Janet was there. I'm surprised she didn't tell you."

"I introduced them," Janet blurted.

"Well, I mean technically . . ." Kayla tried to correct her.

Janet continued, "A bunch of us from Marquette were getting together downtown at The Hideaway. It was one of those meetups that someone put together online."

"Janet was there with Daryll," Craig added.

"And you were there with no one." Janet smiled.

Kayla hit her mark. "Until I found him."

Janet put a finger in the air. "If I recall correctly, you were talking to Daryll. You were telling him about how you and I were in the same sorority together at Marquette."

Kayla nodded and looked at Carole. "That's right, except Janet had graduated my freshman year."

"I was talking with Craig," Janet said, seizing Carole's attention. "We dated in college."

Carole sat up straight. Her face darted from Janet to Kayla and then to Craig. "Such a web! This is exciting. So then what?"

Kayla narrowed her gaze on Carole. "Janet never told you any of this?"

"I only moved in last year." Carole shrugged. "It's not like we hang out every night."

"Oh, I see. I guess," Kayla said. "So, how did you two meet?"

"I answered an ad for a roommate in the Oakdale Reader."

Craig looked at Janet, his face begging for an explanation. Carole spoke up first.

"I told you. Jan is very impulsive." Carole laughed. "The other girl's stuff was still there the day I moved in. The bed was still warm!"

"I thought you two had known each other longer than that," Craig said.

"We are kindred spirits. It seems like we've known each other forever," Carole said as she stood to clear her dishes.

"Oh, just leave those." Kayla rose and began collecting utensils. "You guys go in the family room and I'll bring dessert in there."

Craig found a reason to sneak away from the family room. He joined Kayla at the sink. "This was a bad idea," he said.

"I think it's going great." Kayla hustled to rinse the last of the plates.

"Carole is the only one talking." Craig grabbed a large bowl and set it in the basin to soak. "I can't wait for them to leave."

"She's very outgoing."

"Demonstrative."

Craig dried his hands. He reached in the cabinet for coffee cups and placed them on a serving tray. He scowled at Kayla. She answered with a smile and a peck on his cheek. She dried her hands and grabbed the pot of coffee. When they returned to the family room, Carole was standing with her bag slung over her shoulder.

"Where are you guys going?" Kayla stared. "Don't you want coffee?"

"Carole has a prior engagement," Janet explained. "I'm sorry, I forgot to mention that. Don't worry, I'm going to stay."

"Oh my goodness. I'm so sorry. I thought you knew. I have a friend picking me up." Carole affected a frown. She hugged Kayla, who struggled not to scorch her back with the coffee pot. "I will take a quick cup, though."

Kayla poured four cups and Craig handed them out. Kayla raised the cup to Carole and said, "It was very nice to meet you. Thank you for coming tonight."

"Where are you headed?" Craig asked.

"I'm not sure. He's into arthouse film. We'll probably go to the Match Box down on Southport." Carole said.

"He?" Kayla asked.

"Yes, he," Janet answered. "You never know these days, right?"

"Daryll is his name. Isn't that funny?" Carole giggled and looked about. "Very sweet man. Very interesting. We made these plans before your invitation, but I couldn't turn down the opportunity to meet you guys. It was such a pleasure. Thank you."

Craig and Kayla sipped their coffee.

Carole and Janet sipped their coffee.

"Oh, let me get your coat." Kayla set her cup down and ran to the bedroom.

Carole looked to Craig. "Thanks again."

Craig nodded.

Kayla returned with the coat and handed it to Carole. Carole handed her coffee cup to Kayla, put on her coat, and then took the cup back. "Thank you."

Carole took one more sip and set the cup down. "I'm going to wait outside for Daryll. I don't want him to miss it. These places all look so similar, you know?"

"Of course," Craig said. Janet stayed seated as they walked Carole to the door. The door closed and when Craig and Kayla turned, Janet was sobbing.

Craig and Kayla watched her for a moment. Craig cocked his head. "That was awkward. I'm sorry."

"Why did you bring her?" Kayla asked. "You didn't have to bring anyone."

"Well, Kay, now that you're included in my business, I thought you should see it firsthand." Janet wiped the back of her hand across her cheek. She sipped her coffee. "A live demo, just for you."

Kayla stepped closer. "I didn't know. I would never try to embarrass you."

"Oh, I'm not embarrassed. I really wanted you to see it." Janet sipped her coffee. "I like to keep my faults in the light."

Craig walked over and took Carole's place next to Janet on the loveseat. Kayla winced.

"It's not your fault." Craig looked to Kayla as a queue to speak up.

"Everyone goes through rough patches," Kayla hit her mark, forcing the words through a fake smile.

Kayla placed her hand on Janet's shoulder but she shrunk away from the touch. Kayla sharpened her tone. "You know what? You're right."

Janet's eyes narrowed in return. Kayla stood. Janet stood.

"Oh, I know I'm right. I knew what you were up to the moment you invited me. You're so transparent," Janet scoffed. "You can't stand the thought of your man consoling me, so you bring me here and put your perfect relationship on display."

"It's not perfect but it's way better than anything you'll ever have," Kayla seethed.

"Kayla!?" Craig shouted.

Kay hissed and thrust her finger toward Janet's chest, "Stop writing him. Don't talk to him. If you see him at work, walk the other way,"

Janet laughed and smiled. "We'll see."

Kayla marched to the bedroom and marched back with a coat, throwing it at Janet.

Craig passed by Janet's desk on Monday morning.

"She in today?" Craig asked the woman at the nearest desk. He did not know her name.

The woman stared at Craig for a moment. "She already left for the day," she blurted and fixed her gaze on her computer.

"It's not even ten." Craig checked his watch.

The woman shrugged.

Bill Tripp approached from behind. "Craig?"

"Oh, hey Bill. Good morning."

"Can we chat in my office for a minute?"

Craig noticed Anita approach slowly from behind the corner. She didn't look at Craig. Bill Tripp turned and led Craig to his office. Craig looked back and saw Anita following them several steps behind, her head hung low.

Bill Tripp's office was adorned with framed posters and plastic trophies celebrating the company's achievements. There was a framed picture of a team of GPM employees under a palm tree on a sunny beach. Craig spotted his own grinning face beaming from the back of the group. The script along the bottom of the photo read: *Fort Lauderdale Project / 100,000 units completed*

Bill Tripp sat, so Craig did the same. Anita closed the door of the office and stood near it. She looked like she would have happily stood on the ledge outside the office window if she could.

Craig turned to Anita and said, "Before we start, I just want you to know that I didn't tell anybody about the Jeff Bogden incident." Craig turned back to Bill. "I apologize for making that my business. I am not a gossip. Please don't let this reflect poorly on Anita."

"This isn't about Anita, Craig." Bill Tripp frowned. "And it's not about Jeff Bogden. Not exactly."

"What's this about?"

"What is your relationship with Janet Redgrave?"

"I have no relationship with Janet Redgrave," Craig said bluntly but then backtracked. "I mean. We knew each other in college but then drifted apart for a long time. It had been five or six years that I hadn't seen her when she started working here."

Bill Tripp furrowed his brow. He checked the paperwork in front of him. "You referred a person for employment that you hadn't had contact with for six years?"

"No," Craig said and raised both palms. "She put my name down without telling me."

"But you took the bonus payment?"

"We talked about that, Bill. I came straight to you on Thursday night."

Bill Tripp frowned again. He looked up and to the right as if scanning a recording of the evening's conversations in his mind. "Do you know how many people I meet at each of those parties, Craig? I'm sorry but I don't remember that."

Craig sat back in his chair. He put his palms on his knees and looked back and forth. He looked to Anita, who was still staring at the floor. "Alright, I'll return the money. I haven't even cashed the check. I'll go home and get it at lunch."

"That could be helpful," Bill Tripp conceded.

"Great. And while I'm gone, you can ask Janet about how she put my name down without telling me."

"Janet is gone for the day, Craig."

"OK, tomorrow then."

"Janet will be on leave."

"Call her at home, perhaps?" Craig spread his palms open wide to his sides.

Bill Tripp sighed. He pulled a sheet of paper out from his stack like pulling a card from a deck. He reviewed it to make sure he had selected the right one. Once sure, he turned the paper on the desk to face Craig. It was a printout of an email.

. . . There is no such thing as passion without emotion. I give you a sense of passion which you treasure, but you have to accept the full spectrum of emotions that comes with that. I will be angry, I will make you angry, but we will bring each other joy too. Sometimes - like now - you will be sad, and you will struggle with difficult choices. The choice in this case is whether to sacrifice your short-term happiness for our long-term good. It's up to you to decide if that's a worthwhile trade. It's normal to be cautious or even afraid of what lies ahead if you guess wrong. All I can say is that if you take the risk, I just might surprise you with a bigger payoff than you ever imagined . . .

Craig scanned the top and bottom of the message. The header said it was from him. The signature said it was from him.

I love you,
Craig

"This isn't from me."

"Craig, you put us in a tough spot." Bill Tripp pushed himself away from the desk and stood. "You have to understand that we'll need to get to the bottom of this."

"The bottom of what?!" Craig shouted.

"Do you have an intimate relationship with Janet Redgrave?"

"No."

"Have you ever?"

"Jesus Christ." Craig looked to his left and sneered. "We were in college. It was forever ago."

"It's policy, Craig. You have to tell us about these things before they happen." Bill Tripp spoke calmly.

"But this is after it happened!" Craig shouted. He looked to Anita. He was about to play a card he had promised never to play. "Anita, please reason with him."

Anita looked up from the floor with wide eyes.

"Anita is close with Kayla, my companion," Craig pled. "Anita, tell him. Tell him what Kayla has told you, please!"

Anita summoned her voice but reached only a stammer. She cleared her throat. "Craig, you need to cooperate with us here. Once the truth comes out, you'll be fine."

Kayla's boots clomped on the stairs as she entered through the back entrance of the townhouse. She set her bag down and groaned as she bent over to unzip her boots. She removed her heavy coat and two layers of heavy cardigans. She hung each on a separate hook.

"Man, the wind is zipping out there. The hawk is out!" Kayla rubbed her arms with her palms.

Craig sat on a stool at the counter top in the kitchen. "You were right," he said.

"I don't even know what you're talking about, but I love to hear those words." Kayla found a hook in the cubby to hang her bag. She threw her keys on the counter. The heavy key fob landed with a thud.

"Janet set me up."

Kayla laughed. "Told you she was a manipulative bitch."

"You have no idea."

Kayla waved him off. "I'm sorry about Saturday but I'm not, you know? I think you see now that needed to happen. She needed to see where she stands."

"Well, Kay, right now she is standing at home, or maybe somewhere else, I don't know. What I do know is that she's not standing at the office and neither am I."

She looked at her watch. "Hey, you're home early."

"She told Bill Tripp that we've been having an interoffice romance . . . well, actually, that I have been stalking her. He told her that I recruited her to come work at GPM."

"OK, OK, so what though? There's no proof of this. And . . . AND you have the emails! You can show them that she's into chicks," Kayla walked closer to him. "This is just Bill Tripp following policy, you know that."

"They took my computer. They didn't let me back to my desk." Craig put his face in his palms. "And it gets worse."

"Worse how?"

"Janet works in IT. She's like a network wizard or something. She really knows what she's doing."

"So?"

"She doctored the emails. She made them look like love letters from me to her."

Kayla ran to her bag and retrieved her phone.

"What are you doing?"

Kayla ignored him. She brushed by with the phone to her ear. Craig reached for her arm and she yanked herself away.

"What are you doing!?" he yelled. He caught up to her and reached for the phone.

Kayla yanked away again and cradled the phone in both hands near the nape of her neck. "I'm calling Anita."

"You can't. I already put her in a pickle with this."

"You're not telling me who I can and can't call, understand?" Kayla held her stare for emphasis. Without breaking eye contact, she entered the office and closed the door.

Craig returned to the kitchen and made himself some coffee. He sat at the countertop and listened to Kayla's side of the conversation. As best he could tell, the two girlfriends had reached immediate agreement that Craig was a moron and undeserving of their care and consideration. They got serious after that. There were a lot of groans from Kayla. Then there was pleading and yelling, and more pleading. Finally, Kayla must have heard what she needed to hear.

The door to the office opened.

"Thank you. Thank you." Kayla was smiling. "Don't worry. I won't. I won't. I promise."

Kayla set her phone down on the counter. She went to the cabinet and grabbed a mug. She poured herself a cup of coffee and then sat on the stool next to Craig. They both stared straight ahead and sipped their coffees.

Kayla set her cup down. "The way GPM sees it, you invited a sociopath to their doorstep and let her in."

Craig pouted and nodded. He took another sip of coffee.

"Anita made me promise not to say a word, so you have to keep this to yourself."

Craig put his thumb to his index finger, placed them at the corner of his mouth and then zipped from right to left.

"Daryll has a restraining order on Janet."

Craig pouted and nodded again, as though he would accept any revelation as understandable at this point.

"Her girlfriend's name isn't Carole, it's Jeanine." Kayla took another sip. "And she's not her girlfriend, she's her roommate."

This caught Craig's attention. He sat up straight. "If that's true, this whole thing was a setup."

"Not so impulsive after all, huh?"

"Did you tell Anita?"

"Everything." Kayla took another sip of coffee. "You should be fine once the smoke clears, but they have to follow policy."

Craig put both hands on the countertop and then bowed until his forehead lay on the granite. He let out a deep breath and then rose. He turned to Kayla. "Thank you."

"Your colleague won't be so lucky," she said.

"Who?"

"Some guy named Josh."

Ding dong

Kayla looked to Craig. He stood, walked to the door and checked the peephole. Janet stood there waving with a smile. He pulled back from the hole, looked back and forth, and took another look.

"What do you want?" Craig shouted.

"Please let me in, Craig," Janet shouted back.

"Is that her?" Kayla stood.

Craig shouted back. "You shouldn't be here."

"I'm sorry, I made a mess of everything, but I can fix it. Just let me in, please."

Kayla marched to the door. She pulled it open with a flourish and grabbed Janet behind the neck. Kayla yanked her into the home and threw her to the floor.

Janet lay prone with her right arm supporting her from behind and her left hand in the air. "Stop. I know, but please, just wait."

Craig held Kayla back. Kayla screamed, "Why don't you stop, you cunt!"

"I am. I am." Janet rose carefully, with her left arm still on guard in the air. "I panicked. I pulled Craig into my mess. I'm sorry."

"I've got nothing to say to you." Craig shook his head at her. "You shouldn't be here."

"I'm going to come clean with Bill Tripp and tell him what happened."

"What happened?" Craig spread his arms.

Janet gazed at her feet. "Josh and I've been fooling around for a while now."

"What about Carole?" Kayla asked.

"Oh, give it a rest would you, Kay? You're not in Ohio anymore. Shit gets complicated."

"They say she's your roommate, not your lover, you know?" Craig challenged her.

"Who's 'they,' Craig?" Janet asked.

"And her name is Jeanine." Kayla piled on before he could answer.

Janet began to sob. She fell to her knees and put her face in her hands. She lifted her head and her eyes were deep red. Her mouth was a deep, scowling frown with spittle at one corner. "Do you have any idea what it's like?" She looked back and forth at the two of them. "My parents are Bible beaters, my friends from college are all married with kids and they'd think I'm a freak. The company says they're progressive, but all the execs are fat, pink men from the South."

Kayla's expression did not change, but Craig pitied Janet. "Your business is your business, but I tried to help you. Why did you burn me?"

Janet struggled to her feet and composed herself. "I'm sorry about this. This is embarrassing. God, I'm a mess."

"Maybe you should talk to someone," Kayla suggested, "someone other than Craig."

Suddenly Janet stood stock straight. She stiffened her neck and held her head so high she was looking down her nose at Kayla. Her face burned red and any trace of tears was scorched away.

"I'll talk to whomever I want," Janet yelled.

Bam

The doorknob of their front door shot through the air and tumbled across the floor until it bounced off a wall. The door swung open and Carole entered, a mallet in her hand.

A sonic void of stunned silence expanded like a crystal bubble, then shattered when Craig finally uttered, "It was open."

Carole held the mallet at her chest like she was holding a microphone. She pointed to Kayla. "You, take me to the garage."

"The fuck I will."

Carole raised the hammer and then dropped to one knee like she was genuflecting. The mallet head smashed the toes on Kayla's left foot.

"What the fu . . ." Craig began but was interrupted by the piercing pain of the mallet against his right knee.

Kayla howled. Craig moaned and rolled on the floor.

Janet produced two rolls of duct tape and passed one to Carole. They wrapped Kayla and Craig in thick, silver ribbons of tape. Their arms were bound and their mouths were gagged. Then they used plastic zip ties to bind their wrists and ankles.

"I told you she was impulsive." Carole swung the mallet and breathed heavily. She strolled to Janet and caressed her cheek. Their lips met and they shared a long, deep kiss. Carole broke away and looked down at Craig. "This was meant for Josh, you know?"

Kayla's eyes were red with tears. Craig lay stunned.

"We had all kinds of fun in store for Josh, but Kayla threw a wrench in the plans with her dinner invitation." Carole reached down and grabbed Kayla by the wrists. She yanked her to her feet. Kayla sobbed and groaned and then sobbed again.

"I wasn't completely sure, but then you followed through at work." Janet put her finger beneath Craig's chin and lifted his face to hers. "That's when I decided."

"See? Impulsive." Carole giggled.

Carole looked around the townhome and made her best guess as to which door led to the garage below. She made her choice and dragged Kayla toward the door, grabbing both sets of keys from the counter along the way. When they reached the door, Carole yanked it open and smashed it into Kayla's head, knocking her nearly senseless.

"Ta-ta." Carole waved to Craig and then pushed Kayla down the stairs

Janet circled Craig, the heels of her boots clomping on the cherry wood floor.

Click Thomp

Click Thomp

"Do you remember when Daryll left me? When he left me for that bitch, Carole?"

Craig looked up from the floor. His eyelids sagged. The top edge of the tape ran up to his nostrils and snot pooled where the edge of the tape met his nose. Craig shook his head no.

"I can't see Daryll anymore. Did you know that?"

Craig shook his head again. He put his head down on the floor.

Janet jabbed Craig's knee with a little kick.

Craig cried out through the tape, but it changed to an angry growl. He glared at Janet.

"Oh, do you have something to tell me?" Janet squatted down so she was face to face with Craig. "You're a sweet boy."

Janet tried to place a soft kiss on Craig's forehead but he jerked his head away.

"Do you remember when *you* left me Craig? When we were in college?"

Craig stared back at her, stone faced.

"Do you remember that girl? The Asian girl?"

Craig shook his head.

"No?" Janet stood. "Her name was Carole. Isn't that funny?"

Janet smiled and her eyes lit with excitement. And she held that face for so long it became unnatural.

"I'm going to call you Daryll," Janet told him, still smiling.

Carole ascended the stairs from the garage.

Clomp Clomp Clomp

The door opened. "She's wrapped up tighter than a kielbasa!" She was as bubbly as the Carole who Craig met on Saturday night.

"Go in the kitchen and find a nice knife," Janet told Carole. When Janet looked back at Craig, her smile was gone. Her face was blank and her eyes were focusing on nothing at all, like a blind person with cloudy, useless eyes.

Carole fussed around the kitchen until she found the butcher's block. "Oooh, how about these?"

Carole raised a pair of twelve-inch kitchen scissors. They were heavy, stainless-steel shears designed to cut through meat and bones.

"Bring them here."

Carole handed the shears to Janet.

Craig moaned through the tape. "Naah, nuhhh, nuhhhh." He exhaled from his nose like a bull and his snot shot to the floor. Craig started to prop himself up, but Carole caught him, flipped him over and sat on his back. She plucked off his socks and flung them over her shoulders.

Janet cut through the cuff of Craig's slacks and then dragged the bottom blade up his pant leg. The blade sliced through the fabric with ease. She repeated the process on the other leg and cut all the way to the waist. She had to use both hands to cut through Craig's leather belt. She pulled the shredded pants away from his body.

Other than his swollen knee, Craig's legs were pale, and they nearly matched his white briefs. He squirmed to hide his exposure. Carole smacked the back of his thigh playfully. Craig groaned and then growled in response.

Janet set to cutting off Craig's sweater and t-shirt. When she was finished, Carole rose, and they admired their specimen. While his legs were pale white, his torso was pink. His skin was flush with adrenaline and terror and anger. Craig snarled and kicked at them with his bound legs.

Carole pounced on him like a cattle rustler and bound his legs even tighter with the duct tape. Craig cried in pain.

Carole rose. She and Janet grabbed Craig below the armpits and dragged him to the couch. They hoisted him so that he lay on the couch from the waist up. Then they grabbed his legs and swung them onto the couch.

Craig began to twist but when Janet menaced him with the shears, he went still. As she opened the blades, they made a sound like a sword being unsheathed.

Shhhwinnngggg

Craig only had one garment left. When he felt the cold steel of the shears against his inner thigh, he began to tremble.

"Be still, Daryll. Be still," Janet told him.

Craig began to mumble words from behind the tape.

"Do you have something to say, Daryll?" Janet stared into his eyes as she cut his briefs from his body.

Craig mumbled and moaned again.

Janet took his scrotum in her hand and yanked down. Craig's head arched back in pain, but he kept his lower quarters still. Janet brought the open blades around his sack. The blades touched his skin and all the hairs on his body rose to attention.

"Take off the tape, Carole." Janet stared again at Craig. "Don't scream, Daryll."

Carole propped Craig's head up on the arm of the couch. Janet was still poised with the shears. Carole found an edge and unwound the tape from around Craig's head. When she reached the end, she couldn't remove the part of the tape that was stuck to his long hair so the whole strand hung from his head. He looked like an unwrapped mummy.

Craig breathed deeply from his mouth. Then he began to cry.

Janet pressed the steel of the scissors against his skin. "What if Carole saw you like this?"

Craig looked up at Carole. "Who?"

"Not that Carole. The Carole in your car. Your girlfriend," Janet told him. She brought the shears to his neck.

"Her name is Kayla." Craig focused on the tip of the shears pointed at his throat.

"I am going to call her Carole."

"What did you do to her?"

Carole stood beside him holding his car keys in her hand. "Nothing yet, except for breaking a few little bones."

"Why are you doing this?"

Janet's face went blank again. She looked robotic. She held out her hand and Carole put the keys in it. Janet pressed a button on the key fob and the car below rumbled to life, inside the garage. She straddled Craig and leaned in close. She opened the blades around his throat. She leaned close to his ear. "No more Carole."

Craig couldn't process anything but pain and fear. He shot a glance at the Carole in the room.

Carole noticed. "Oh, me? You're wondering about me, aren't you?"

Carole pushed Janet aside. She held the mallet in her hand. "I told you, we're kindred spirits. But I live by a different mantra."

Carole hopped on the bed and straddled Craig across the waist. She raised the mallet above her head. "No more Daryll."

The detail on the hammer's head was vivid.

Carbon Steel 8lb.

Carbon Steel 8lb.

Carbon Steel 8lb.

Crunch

2

JUST JAMES

"You can't just scream at a child, James," Brenda told her brother.

"Get lost, he yelled at me first." James nursed his left eye with his cold beer.

"He's eleven."

"I'm his uncle."

"And I'm his mother. And Ray is his father."

James and Brenda Butterfield sat on the deck outside her two-bedroom home in Venice, California. The modest home was 800 square feet in size and the fenced-in yard to the side added another 200 square feet to the property.

The sliding door opened to a small deck where James and Brenda sat. Ray stepped outside. "Jimmy, I'm sorry," he said.

"Who throws a basketball like that inside the house, huh?" James scolded. "It's like a racquetball court in there. You could have brained my nana."

"Dude, in my family, you don't scream at another man's child."

"He yelled at me first!" James pointed at Ray.

"Dude, you told him there's no such thing as Santa—two weeks before Christmas."

Brenda looked askance at her brother.

"Not true. He asked me if I believed in Santa and I told him no." James took a sip of his beer. "Then I told him the elves he sees on TV are dwarves who were abandoned to the studios by their parents. They live on the backlots. All of this is fact. You can look it up."

"Dude," Ray said, shaking his head, "he's eleven."

"I'm out of here." James stood and pounded his beer. "I'm walking down to the beach."

"We're doing the piñata in an hour," Brenda pled.

"Don't break any fixtures." James opened the gate and left. He lit a smoke as he hit the sidewalk and began his trek down to Venice Beach.

It was in the 60s down on the boardwalk and the breeze off the Pacific cut at James' neck. He flipped the collar on his suede coat and lit another smoke. He sat on a bench and watched the passersby, waiting to recognize someone he knew. Vagabonds and muscle-heads and geriatric hippies meandered in a parade of humanity. Finally, he saw Monique appear at the far north end of the path. Rather, he saw the pack of dogs huffing and striding as they towed her on her skates.

Monique made her living as a dog walker in Venice. At the moment, she held harness to five dogs of various shape, size and stripe. She was on call to some of the celebrities who kept homes in Venice. This fact alone made her an interesting partner for conversation. What was even more fascinating was that she believed she received messages from each dog whenever she grabbed a leash.

"Hey, Mo. Monique. What's good?" James stood and waved as she approached.

Monique dropped a heel to activate the brakes on her inline skates.

"Hey, Jimmy. I thought you were back east." Monique dropped her backpack from one shoulder while still holding five leashes in one hand. James reached out to take the bundle from her but she waved him off.

"I needed to get back home. Find some work." James took a step away and smashed out his smoke beneath his toe.

"Nashville not for you?" Monique pulled out five plastic bowls and un-nested them from each other. When she placed them on the ground, the dogs nuzzled at them so they moved around like amoeba. Monique pulled a two-liter water bottle from the backpack and poured three fingers of water in each bowl. The two Havanese fought over one bowl until one surrendered and found another. The tiny Dachshund wormed his snout in with the massive Bernese, who either didn't notice or didn't care. The Chocolate Lab trotted around like an oblivious idiot while the rest of the dogs enjoyed their refreshments.

"It wasn't my scene, you know? I felt like a fraud."

"It's a shame about Nora." Monique handed the leashes to James. She went to the nearest water fountain and refilled her two-liter bottle. The Chocolate Lab took a dump behind the bench.

"Yeah, I gave it a shot, but it wasn't working out for me." James caught sight of the Lab's business and winced.

"No, I'm talking about her thing, you know? Her getting sick."

"Nah, I didn't hear anything about that."

Monique walked back toward James. She slipped the water bottle back in her pack. "Here, hand me Otto."

"Which one's Otto?"

"The Dachshund."

"What's a Dachshund?"

"The wiener dog."

James handed Otto's leash to Monique. As she gripped the red loop, she closed her eyes. The wind from the ocean blew at the hems of her long red skirt. A lock of brown air blew across her face but she left it there, unperturbed. "Otto says he heard his owners talking about Nora. They know her agent. She's sad. She made herself sick."

"Ha, they know John Klein? That guy hates me. No wonder I didn't hear about it."

The Chocolate Lab turned and kicked grass on his dirty business and then rejoined the group of dogs. He lapped at a water dish and made a slobbery mess of his face.

"She had to cancel some shows."

"Listen, Monique, I appreciate the update but, like I said, I'm over that." James looked out over the horizon and squinted. "Jimmy Butterfield took a shot at the country crossover and it didn't work out."

She handed Otto back to James. He handed her the leashes for the two tiny Havanese dogs. "Here, what do these little ladies have to say?"

"Jimmy Butterfield?" the receptionist called out.

James approached her desk. "Actually, it's James now."

"James Butterfield?" The woman readied her pen to correct the name on her pad.

"No, just James," he told her.

"Just James?"

"Yes, just James."

She scribbled out his last name on her pad. She turned to the keyboard. "Hold on. I need a last name for the system. I can't leave that field blank."

"Fine, put B in there."

She typed a B. "Nope, can't be one letter."

"Try Bu."

"Nope." She added a T. "Oh, that works."

"You put me in there as James But?"

The woman threw up her hands in mock frustration.

"Just put Butterfield, just put Butterfield." James wiped at his forehead with his palm.

The woman jabbed at the keys and completed the names. She looked up at James with a wide, fake smile. "Mr. Templeton is waiting for you."

"Thank you." James made his way past her desk.

The woman looked at her monitor and muttered, "Just James is already taken, you dolt."

James knocked at Harry Templeton's door and it opened under the force of his rapping.

"Hey, Harry."

"Jimmy Butterfield!" Harry greeted him from behind his desk. He did not stand.

James reached across the desk to shake Harry's hand. He did not correct him about his name.

"I came as soon as I could, Harry."

"I'm sure you did, Jimmy." Harry shook his head and flashed a smile. Hanging on the wall behind him were photos of Harry with numerous celebrities. All of them were at the top of the industry, at that moment. On the walls to the left and right were pictures of Harry with other celebrities. These stars had faded, hence their relegation to the lateral walls.

James leaned forward in his chair. "You called me in because you want to make sure I understand something, and I know that."

"And what is it that I want you to understand Jimmy?"

"I owe you money."

"Good. Elaborate, please."

"You want that money."

"You're on a roll."

"I need to give you that money."

"Or?"

"Something bad is going to happen."

Harry let out a bellowing laugh and dropped his palm on his desk.

Bam

"Jimmy! I'm not a thug!" Harry looked away as if he was embarrassed. "I'm your agent."

"I don't have the money, Harry," James told him plainly. "I need work."

"What happened to that sweet gig I set up with Nora Lynn? Klein tells me you fucked that all up?"

"It wasn't for me. Nashville's not my style."

Harry nodded his head and dwelled on the response, "Jimmy, do you know what a carbuncle is?"

"A what?"

"A carbuncle; do you know what it is?" Harry waited a moment and then continued. "You see this?" Harry sat up, reached down and produced a donut shaped cushion from beneath his tuchus.

James nodded and stared but made no expression. His punishment was coming. He just wanted to get on with it. He fixed his stare on a picture of Harry sitting in a booth with some studio head. Harry wore a shiny suit and the same knowing smile that he showed when James first sat down.

"A carbuncle is a collection of inflamed hair follicles, James. Kind of like a pimple, but a gang of them," Harry explained. "I have a carbuncle on my taint."

"Your taint?"

"Yes, Jimmy, my taint. You know? That flap of skin between your balls and your asshole? It ain't your balls and it ain't your ass?"

"Yes, I know the expression but how the hell did that happen?" James asked.

"In-grown hair; too much time on the stationary bike." Harry laughed. "I thought I had an infected hernia or something. I went into the local pharmacy and gave them a look. They said they'd have me arrested if I ever came back. I go all the way down to Century City to get my prescriptions filled now."

James slunk in his chair and dropped his forehead to his palm as Harry cackled. A slow, rumbling laugh percolated in his own belly. The humor of the situation blossomed within him and he joined his agent in a chuckle. Almost as soon as James joined in his laughter, Harry's face turned serious and he stopped laughing.

"That's what you are, Jimmy. You're a carbuncle on my taint. You're an infected nest of rank hair festering between my balls and asshole." Harry's face turned red and he screamed. "I feel you pulsing every time I sit and you sting with every step I take!"

James sat up straight and took it.

"I want to reach down and squeeze you till you pop. I want to watch your insides squirt out onto the floor, but I can't do that. You're an infection. That'll just make things worse. I have to treat you. I have to treat you and wait." The crimson flush faded. Harry caught his breath. He sat back and opened the plastic bottle of water that was on his desk. He tipped his head back and downed it in a straight shot. He crumpled up the bottle and threw it at James.

James stood still and let the bottle bounce off his chest.

"I'm not your agent anymore."

"I need to make some money to pay you back."

"I can take whatever you make, however you make it. Read your contract. That was an advance on future revenue. It doesn't stipulate how you make the money."

James sat dumbfounded. "I can't get another agent after working with you."

"No shit." Harry smiled the same knowing smile. He was perfectly calm again. "Listen, kiddo, maybe you can make something from that gig with Nora Lynn. I heard she slipped pretty hard on the meds when she went back home. Inside info on that could get you some coin."

"I'll take anything. Get me some commercials in China, I don't care. Anything." James placed his palms together.

Harry repositioned the doughnut cushion under his ass. His face crumpled with discomfort. "Boner meds," he said.

"Boner meds?"

"That's right. Boner meds." Harry smiled his smile. "You're going to be the young face of boner meds."

James' face crumpled.

"It just came to me." Harry chuckled to himself. "You're perfect: young and recognizable, somewhat relevant. And no one will be surprised to see you plugging boner pills."

James pled some more. "Harry, thank you, but when I said anything, I meant . . ."

Harry cut him off. "I've got full discretion on filling this one. It's yours. It pays, too; one-hundred K for three spots."

James looked up. "I guess I could . . ." he began but trailed off. "Nah. Nah, nah, nah, nah."

"Nah, nah, nah, my aching ass!" Harry screamed. He pointed at James. "They're ready for the read-through as soon as I send them a guy. You'll be there tomorrow."

"Harry, tomorrow's tough for me."

Harry's face stayed flush but he lowered his voice. "You owe me sixty-five thousand dollars, you no-talent, has-been cocksucker. At the end of the month it'll be seventy thousand. I don't give a shit how you get it, but you are doing that read-through."

Scene: Upbeat pop music plays in a hip, urban lounge setting. Men and women dance on a crowded dance floor. Camera pans in on James and Lisa.

James (young male patient): I love to dance to this song.

Lisa (female interest): I'd like to do a different dance.

(Music stops.) Everyone freezes and fades to grey except for James. Tight focus on James' face.

Narrator (overdubbed): Uh oh, does James have the moves? Can James . . . bust a move?

James winks and flashes a sly smile.

(Music changes to a funky, syncopated track with heavy wah effect.) Camera pans back to show James and Lisa in bedroom. James has arm slung low around Lisa's back. They undulate in rhythm as they creep closer to the edge of the bed.

Narrator (overdubbed): Looks like James has Rigidon, so he can dance all night long.

Tight focus on James' face. James winks and flashes a sly smile.

"That's it?" James flips the page over to look for more lines on the other side of the script.

The director sat at the head of the long conference table. He lifted his glasses off the bridge of his nose and placed them on top of his head. "Were you expecting a soliloquy?"

"Well, I was told it was a forty-five-second spot." James looked around the conference room at the pathetic faces of the crew assigned to the project. Aside from the director, there was a line producer, two folks from the advertising agency and numerous assistants. There was also the woman playing Lisa and a handsome young actor who had yet to reveal his purpose.

"The balance of time is for disclaimers and side effects," the director shrugged.

"What kind of side effects?" James asked.

"Are you thinking about taking some?" The woman playing Lisa giggled.

"Only if I had to bang you."

The room erupted and the woman shrunk.

The director's assistant leafed through her papers, found a page and read. "Looks like this stuff hits you below the waist one way or another: irritable bowel, loose stool, spastic colon, flatulence."

"Wonderful," James quipped.

"All right, shall we run through the next spot?" the director asked.

"Yes, let's just get through this, please." James gripped the base of his nose with his fingers and then rubbed his eyes.

One of the assistants shuffled through her folders to find the script for the second spot. The handsome young man leaned across the table and spoke to James, "I loved you in 'Whispering Hills'."

James pulled his fingers from his eyes and looked at him. "Were you watching it from the womb? I was just a boy back then."

The young man looked like he may have been old enough to drink. He had feather-light blonde hair and blue eyes. He wore a jean jacket over a t-shirt. He received a stack of scripts from the assistant, took one and passed the stack down. "I love classic TV," he told James.

"Ha, thanks." James smirked.

James received his copy of the script and read the cover: Alternative Spot for Rigidon

"I'm David," the man said and reached across the table to shake James' hand.

"James."

"Of course."

At that moment it occurred to James that his character was actually named James; it wasn't just a placeholder for him in the script. James raised the sheet of paper in his hand and looked to the director. "Hey, Brent, do we really have to call this guy James."

"Talk to creative." The director and pointed to the two suits at the far end of the table.

"It tested well," one of the suits from the ad agency answered quickly.

"It's kind of, on the nose, don't you think?" James reasoned.

"It tested well," the director shrugged and put his face into the script.

James squeezed the bridge of his nose and rubbed his eyes again. He took the script, slapped it on the table and tore off the cover page. He adjusted the sole page of dialogue squarely before himself.

Scene: Bright sunny day in a public park. A man tosses a Frisbee to his dog. The dog misses it and it lands near James (young male patient). James picks up the Frisbee and holds it. The dog approaches and James pets him with affection. He catches the eye of the dog's owner and smiles at him. He throws the Frisbee to the owner and the dog chases after it.

James: That's a handsome boy.

Philip (male interest) I was thinking the same thing.

Camera focuses tightly on James. James winks and flashes a sly smile.

"Whoa. Whoa, whoa, whoa." James lifted his hands from the table and pushed himself away. "Guys, I was just doing work in Nashville. This isn't going to mesh with my image."

"Relax, James. This one will only run in three regions: New York, Miami and California," the director told him.

James peered at Brent. He waited for a longer, better assurance. "You're kidding right?"

"Kidding?" Brent stared back at James. "Do you want work, James? Yes or no?"

"Give the gay spot to someone else. I'll take the other two." He pushed the script away from himself. It caught air and floated across the table toward David, who looked at James with pity.

The guys from the ad agency looked at each other. The first suit spoke, "We are targeting the younger demographic. They're sexual pioneers. They're undefined. Anything is game."

The other suit spoke, "James is what's called polyamorous. It's a new thing. He has to be the protagonist for all three spots or the message will be muddied."

David pushed the script back toward James. "Work is work man, come on."

James grabbed the script and flipped it around. "I'll give you muddied. I bet you guys love it muddied," he grumbled.

(Soft music starts.) James and Philip walk near each other in the park. The dog jumps between them playfully.

Narrator (overdubbed): Looks like James fetched himself a new friend at the park. But will he have a treat for him once they get home?

James winks and flashes a sly smile.

(Music changes to a slow, soulful track with light organ.) Camera focuses on a vase of flowers on a nightstand. In the background (out of focus), two people laugh and cavort beneath the sheets of a bed.

Narrator (overdubbed): Looks like James has Rigidon, so he can play all night long.

Tight focus on James' face. James winks and flashes a sly smile.

"Fuuuuuuuck," James groaned and tilted his head back. He placed both palms on his face.

David offered some perspective. "You said it yourself. It's like a twenty-second spot."

"Yeah, the last twenty seconds of my career."

"You could redefine yourself. The street could see this as brave." The director tried.

"Can we take lunch?" James stood as he asked.

"Sure, James." The director sympathized.

James left his scripts at his spot at the table and walked out. Everyone else stayed in their places.

The director's assistant leaned into the director's ear. "This is where we always lose them."

"Get Harry on the phone. We may need to up the pay on this one."

Brenda Butterfield cracked open a beer and handed it to her brother. "Search your heart."

James pitched the beer bottle back and took a long swallow. Then he set the bottle down and sighed. "What the fuck does that even mean?"

They were in Brenda's backyard in Venice. It was late afternoon. The sun's pink and orange light peaked through from just above the horizon. It was majestic.

"Set aside all the distractions you in your mind. Meditate. Once you have your breathing under control, the only thing you'll have left to listen to is your heartbeat. That's when the answer will come to you." She patted her brother on the leg and took a swig of her own beer.

She was five years older than him. They had never been rivals. They had a sister who was two years older than Brenda. Neither of them got along with her. James was Brenda's confidant and she was his beacon.

James put his feet flat on the ground, crossed his arms and shut his eyes.

"Uncross your arms," Brenda told him.

James did so.

"Breath."

James exhaled out his nose.

"Release your tension."

His shoulders slumped. His head tilted forward.

"Even your face. Your face is tight. Let that go."

James' cheeks fell and his jowls hung loose. His mouth dropped into a pout.

"Concentrate on your breathing."

James and Brenda sat silently. The evening breeze off the Pacific came and went with the rhythm of their breathing.

James honed in on his breathing. The bright light in his mind dimmed with each breath he took. Waves of relaxation washed over him. He felt like his brain was suspended in warm gelatin. The light slowly narrowed to a single point, a portal. He advanced to the portal and crossed over.

There was a woman there. She was young and percolated with energy. It was Nora Lynn Donovan, his ex-girlfriend. She laughed and sang and spoke, but no sounds came from her. All James could hear was his heartbeat.

Thump thump

Thump thump

Thump thump

James moved toward her. She moved toward him. Nora Lynn Donovan brought her face to his ear and cupped her hand near his cheek. She was going to tell him something. James leaned in to receive the message.

"James! What's up, man?" Ray appeared from the sliding door heading out to the patio.

James' mind returned to the backyard in Venice. He opened his eyes, still in his trance, to see his brother-in-law twist open a beer for himself. The warm glow of the meditative state lingered, and he didn't want to say anything to break its flow.

"James, partner, what's up?" Ray rubbed James' shoulder.

"We were meditating," Brenda said without opening her eyes.

"Oh, sorry, bro. Didn't mean to rock your chill state." Ray turned to go back inside just as his son, Jeffrey, squeezed through the opening in the sliding door.

"Hi, Uncle Jimmy," he said as he jumped into James' arms.

"Hey, buddy."

"What were you doing out here?"

"Looking for answers, buddy, looking for answers."

Jeffrey looked around the tiny yard. He couldn't kick a ball back there without it going over the fence. "I don't think you'll find much back here, Uncle Jimmy."

The adults laughed together. Jeffrey looked puzzled.

"It's OK, buddy. I think I found it already."

The sliding door to the patio was still open and the family's dog trotted out. She was an old Golden Retriever. The hair on her face had gone white. She trotted over to Brenda and dropped her snout onto her lap. Brenda stroked her behind her ear and her tail wagged.

"So where is it, Uncle Jimmy?"

"It's not here. I have to go talk to Otto."

It was Saturday morning and the boardwalk of Venice was a hive of physical activity. Locals ran and skated and biked up and down the pathways. Lanky, lean men hoisted themselves on the bars and rings apparatus on the beach, like acrobats. The muscle-heads arrived at their stations with their belts and hand wraps slung over their massive shoulders. The hippies and freaks were nowhere to be seen—other than those sleeping in gangways and under benches. Venice on Saturday morning was the domain of the jocks.

James found the bench where he had met Monique. He sat and lit a smoke. He popped the plastic top off his coffee cup and steam erupted from the surface of the brown elixir. He took a drag from his smoke and peered north up the boardwalk toward Santa Monica. He turned his head and exhaled a grey plume. He looked south down the boardwalk. He did not see any sign of Monique.

It was chilly. James wore boots, jeans, a flannel shirt, and a jean jacket with wool lining. The brim of his blue Dodgers cap was pulled too low, so he pushed it up with his finger to get a better view up and down the pathway.

There she was, coming from the north. Monique must have taken the dogs up to the pier, now she was on her return trip.

James counted the dogs. There were six: the Chocolate Lab, the Bernese, the two Havanese and a couple mutts he couldn't distinguish. Where was Otto?

"Hey, Monique!" James shouted and waved.

"Hey, James!" Monique waved back with her free hand. She was dressed light for the cool morning, but her face was flushed red with warmth.

"Where's Otto?" James cut straight to the point.

Monique deftly extracted one red leash from her bundle and Otto emerged from beneath the Bernese.

"Oh, thank God." James exhaled his last drag and smashed out his smoke.

Monique handed James the bundle of leashes and commenced with her routine of filling the dogs' bowls from her water bottle. The Chocolate Lab trotted behind the bench and laid eight inches of coil in the dirt.

"What's wrong? What's bothering you?"

"I need to talk to Otto."

Monique smiled and the dimples on her happy, Irish face made deep crevices on her cheeks. She quietly continued filling the water dishes. She finished and then walked over to the water fountain to refill her bottle.

"I like you, James. Most people don't indulge me like you do." Monique sat next to James and rubbed the top of his cap like she was petting a dog.

James crouched his head to accept the affection. He watched the dogs lap at their water. "Why don't you just fill the bowls straight from the fountain instead of emptying out the filled bottle?"

"I can only fill one at a time that way. If I set just one down, they will all crowd around and fight over it."

"I figured the little ones would just let the big guy there have first dibs."

Monique chuckled. "Oh James, those dogs don't know they're little. You see Bacino there?"

"Which one's that?"

"The Havanese with the brown mask." She pointed to his left side. "He spent a week in the puppy ICU after he attacked a racoon."

"Ballsy."

"Well, no. He doesn't have any of those, anymore."

They laughed together for a moment. Monique reached for Otto and James handed her his leash. "State your business with my wiener."

They laughed even harder. James caught his breath. "I want to know more about Nora."

"Why?"

"I care about her and want to know what happened."

"Why not just call her then?"

James was not expecting this level of intuition from a dog-sitter/dog-seer.

"I just need to know, OK?"

"You were a sweet boy when I first met you." The happiness left Monique's happy face.

James looked away from her. "I'm the same person you met back on that set."

Monique went to her satchel and retrieved a plastic bag. She paced behind the bench to the Chocolate Lab's dirty business. She held Otto's leash. He sniffed at the pile on the ground until she yanked him back.

"Don't you want to let that cool?" James scowled in disgust.

She placed the bag over her hand like a glove. "Shit is shit. Hot or cold. Old or new."

"I'm in a jam, I need some money to pay my agent."

"Still with Harry, huh?" Monique reached down and put her covered hand around the pile of soft, warm dog poo. The feces spread between the creases in the bag that outlined her fingers. "Did he try to put you on the Rigidon gig?"

"How the hell do you know this?"

"Rowdy told me." She pointed to a tawny mutt that looked like it was part Pit Bull.

"Listen Monique, I've never been a perfect person, but I haven't changed either. And I haven't done anything wrong."

She held the pile of shit aloft in her right hand. "Not yet."

James recoiled as she walked back from behind the bench and crossed the path to the nearest garbage can. "I'm calling the media no matter what. I'm going to do right by Nora. I'll keep it positive, you know, supportive."

"So go ahead then."

"I can't just cold call them with that. That's too lean. I need to give them the big story, you know, about her getting sick, as you put it." James made quotes in the air with his fingers as best he could with the leashes in his hand.

"I dunno." Monique smacked her hand on her thigh, seemingly to release any poop particles that may have lingered. Otto jumped up and nipped at her, thinking she wanted to play.

"I'm in a pinch, Mo. I mean, come on, look at yourself right now." James raised the knot of leash handles towards her. "Is this what you want to be doing for work?"

"Actually I enjoy this. It's good exercise and I enjoy the company. Usually."

"Wouldn't you rather be acting still? Choosing the parts you take? Honing your craft?"

"I do act. I'm part of a little theatre workshop in Hermosa. We hold classes for new actors every night and have reviews on the weekends. I'm on the staff and a part owner."

James cocked his back. "I had no idea."

"No idea about what? That a boardwalk weirdo could be capable of more than a side hustle?" Monique pointed to the dogs. "Stop chasing fame, James. You will never be relevant in this town. You had a couple high-profile gigs but your sun has set. Don't go chasing the moon now."

James raised his hands in surrender. "All I wanted was to talk to Otto."

Monique nodded. "I'm sorry, I wasn't entitled and you didn't deserve that."

"Please?"

Monique sat next to James on the bench. She slapped her lap and Otto jumped onto her. The other dogs crowded around her jealously but James pulled them away to give her space.

Monique closed her eyes and stroked Otto's wiry coat. "He says she left a letter and then pounded a handful of Oxy. She washed it down with a jammy Cabernet."

"Where did this happen? Nashville?"

"No, she was at home for Thanksgiving, at her parent's house."

"Does he know why she did it?"

"He says it had nothing to do with you." She opened one eye and looked at James. "She cancelled the rest of her shows though. She's going to stay home for a while, spend time with her family and old friends."

"What did John Klein have to say about that?" James asked about her agent.

"He wants Nora working, obviously."

"That guy's a fucking jerk."

Monique opened her one eye again. "Otto says he's good friends with his masters."

"Tell Otto I'm sorry."

"He can hear you just fine."

James reached over and pet the dog, "I'm sorry, Otto."

The dog wagged his tail and turned to give James his belly.

"Hey, Otto, do you think I should give Nora a call?"

Monique smiled. "Otto thinks she would probably like that."

Volatility – Hollywood's Premier Insider Outlet

Nora Lynn Overdose Shocker: America's sweetheart popstar pops pills 'til she pukes

Sources tell Volatility magazine that the reason for Nora Lynn Donovan's cancelled shows is an overdose of pain medication. This contradicts the account from her manager, John Klein, who told outlets that Nora Lynn was suffering from exhaustion and the flu.
Our sources tell us that Miss Donovan ingested large quantities of the prescription pain medication, Oxycontin, and then mixed the dose with

alcohol. Miss Donovan was at her parent's home in Clifton, Michigan at the time of the incident.

Our sources contend that John Klein has driven Nora Lynn into a breakdown, thanks to a grueling recording schedule and endless tour. Indeed, a review of Nora Lynn's schedule shows she had not taken a significant break for more than two years. Mr. Klein declined comment on this story.

James knew who was calling the second he heard the phone rang. The story was the banner headline on Volatility daily magazine that Monday morning—both the print and digital versions. James let it ring a couple times as he lit a smoke and stepped out on the sidewalk. "Hello," he said and exhaled a long, cloudy dragon of smoke.

"You little cocksucker, I didn't think you'd actually do it." It was Harry, his erstwhile agent.

"Do what?" James took another drag.

"Dish on Nora to that rag."

"Wasn't me," James told him and that was the truth. He had spoken to Nora, but he wasn't the source of the story. He knew that wouldn't matter. The timing looked awful. Monique would think he did it. Nora would think he did it. Neither of them would be calling, but he knew Harry would call. He'd be looking for his money.

"HA! OK, Jimmy." Harry scoffed but then he turned sweet. "Listen, I'm sorry about those things I said last week. I have self-esteem issues and I have to insult people to feel better about myself."

"Apology accepted."

"Now, where's my money?"

"I don't have it. I wasn't the source."

There was silence on the line. James smoked his cigarette and stared down the boulevard in front of his motel. He imagined Harry playing a game of mental chess, trying to decide his next move. He imagined Harry thinking about all the bums patrolling Venice and how that was probably James' destiny; a broke bum, incapable of paying him back.

"I got good feedback from Brent about you," Harry chose his play.

"Oh yeah?"

"He loved your work on the Rigidon spots. The pharma guys did, too. They insist on having you, only you."

"How bad do they want me?" James bit.

"They'll go to $150,000."

James flicked his smoke into the street. "One-hundred-and-fifty-thousand dollars for three, 20-second spots?"

"One hundred and fifty thousand for a minute of your time, Jimmy."

"How is that possible?"

"It's pharma, Jimmy. They have more money than God."

There was another pause and then Harry dropped some gravy on top. "Listen, Jimmy, you take this, give me fifty grand and we'll call it square. You walk away with a hundred large."

"That's very generous of you."

"Damn right."

James lit another smoke. He looked south down the boulevard. He watched the cars head to who knows where with people going to do who knows what. He looked north and did the same.

"Jimmy? Jimmy, I ain't got all day." Harry said.

"I do," James replied.

"Jimmy, buddy, you're trying my fucking patience here."

"I remember when I was a kid and my parents told me to live in the moment, but all I wanted to do was think about the future," James pondered aloud. "Well, now I'm an adult and all I do is worry about tomorrow."

"Jimmy, how about you put one hundred thousand dollars in your pocket today? How about that?"

James turned and looked at the rusting marquee of the Boulevard Motel. He looked at the lot of cars, a couple of which weren't going anywhere under their own power ever again.

"I'll do it if you'll be my agent again; if you get me another gig."

"For Chrissakes, Jimmy, you really are the carbuncle on my ass, you know that?"

"How's that going, by the way?"

"It popped on Saturday, actually. I was at dinner with a bunch of studio pricks. I rocked in my chair to reach for some butter and, bam, the fucker exploded right there in my drawers. Felt the puss ooze down my leg. Best night out all year."

"That's disgusting."

"Whatever, you asked." Harry said. "All right, enough of that. What kind of gig you lookin' for?"

3

HE'LL NEVER THINK TO ASK

"Talk is cheap," says the man in blue, "Except for lies, those will cost you,"

"Why won't you tell me your last name?" Doyle fusses with the napkin on her lap.

The man checks his watch. "We already covered that."

A voice from behind the curtain asks, "Mi scusi, signora, may I interrupt?"

"Yes." Doyle reaches to draw the curtain back with her left hand. Chefs scurry from station to station behind the waiter as he places the curtains in the hook holds on each side of the private booth inside the kitchen.

The waiter places a plate of risotto with scallops and prawns in front of Doyle. He places another risotto dish with truffles in front of the man in blue. He accepts a light dusting of fresh parmesan on his plate but none is offered to Doyle.

"Why were you in Cuba?" The man in blue turns the risotto with his spoon to mix the cheese into the dish. Steam billows up and black truffle shavings pierce the surface.

"To learn Spanish." Doyle turns her risotto as well. A puff of steam distorts her face.

"That seems tedious and expensive."

"Have you ever been to Cuba?"

"Again, you are not paying me to answer your questions."

"I need to know I can trust you." Doyle pets the designer purse resting at the side of her chair.

"Miss Doyle, I know why we're eating in the kitchen," the man in blue says. He places a morsel of risotto on the tip of his spoon. He brings it to his mouth, gives the slightest blow and gently places it on the tip of his tongue.

"Because I'm cautious and connected and discreet." Doyle scoops a heaping pile of risotto on her spoon and jams it into her mouth. She quickly chews and swallows. "And so are you. That's why Kim put us in touch. I trust her and she trusts you, but there's no associative property when it comes to what I'm asking you to do."

"Associative property? Are you a math teacher, Miss Doyle?"

"You've heard enough about me."

The man in blue smiles to himself and rearranges the napkin on his lap. "Still, Cuba? We live in Miami. You can't throw a bunuelo without hitting a Cubana around here . . . or a Cubano?"

Doyle stabs her spoon into the middle of her bowl and it stands straight up. "There are certain themes that must be adhered to if we wish to maintain authenticity."

"Fastidious, I appreciate that. And I agree, details are what insulate the lie from the truth." The man in blue nods. "But still, this is Miami."

"That's the point. The Cubans here are not the same. These are the old aristocrats, the elitist American puppets the people rose up against."

"Are you a socialist?"

Doyle shakes her head and grabs the spoon from her dish. She shakes it ever so slightly and a single ort is jettisoned onto the taut, white tablecloth. "My husband will recognize the difference. We can't do this at any old place on Calle Ocho."

"Miss Doyle, I don't understand why it has to be done in public at all." The man raises his palms toward Doyle and makes a plaintive face.

Doyle points the spoon at the man in blue. "My husband is sharp. If there is any clumsy detail, he will sniff it out and he won't show."

"Still, why in public?"

"Do you think he's just going to sit down to dinner with you, a complete stranger?" Doyle places the spoon down and takes a sip of her white wine.

"Why not in your home?"

"Because then I would have to be in on it."

The man chortles, "Oh, Miss Doyle, you are in on it."

"I can't know anything more than the simplest of details. I will never stand up to questioning."

"I think I agree." The man sips his wine. "How about a church?"

Doyle's face squeezes and her eyes draw to sharp blades. "What's wrong with you?"

"Your husband is religious, correct?"

"He's Catholic, of course, but that's more by identity than by practice."

"I mean if a colleague invites him to a wedding or a baptism, he will attend, correct?"

The waiter clears his throat to announce his presence. "Will our guests be enjoying a second course this evening?"

"Bring the porchetta please, and a bottle of the 1997 Brunello," Doyle tells him.

"Excellent choice," the man in blue says. "You assume I'm a meat-eater, though."

"Who said I was sharing?"

"You must have quite an appetite."

Doyle enjoys another bite of risotto, places her spoon down and takes a large gulp of wine. She sets her glass down and levels her gaze. "How the hell am I supposed to arrange for someone to have a baby or get married just to fit our plans?"

"Miss Doyle, there are baptisms every Sunday afternoon at the cathedral downtown. We pick one and then draft a fake invitation to you and your husband. You can tell him it's the child of a distant cousin, or a coworker or an important civic official. It won't matter. Once we get him to the final destination, he'll never think to ask."

Doyle allows a wide, sinister smile to stretch across her face. "And it's not like we'd go to the service anyway."

The man in blue nods and smiles.

"I'll tell him we need to pop into the reception afterward, just to drop off the gift. He won't question anything." Doyle nods back.

"OK, then. Now, for the Cuban touch?"

"Just take care of what we discussed right now. I'll take care of the romantic touch."

"I am perfectly capable handling that, Miss Doyle," the man in blue pleas, seemingly offended.

Doyle takes the napkin from her lap and wipes her face. She stands, walks to the man's side of the table and leans over to speak directly into his face. "This isn't a fucking Nora Lynn Donovan love song. This is a job. Just get it done."

Doyle reaches into her purse and pulls out a fat, white envelope. She places it on the table. "Enjoy the porchetta."

"It's such a relief. I don't think I ever felt such a sense of relief in my life." Doyle holds out her champagne flute to toast her friend.

Kim reaches out and touches the rim of her glass to Doyle's.

Ting

"Cheers."

"Cheers."

"It was so grueling, just so grueling, you know? Thank God it's over." Tears well in Doyle's eyes. "I could not have done it without you."

"What did I do?" Kim places her hand to her chest. "My prints aren't on this."

"You found me Manuel." Doyle puts her hand on Kim's shoulder and giggles. "I was such a bitch to him, too."

"Listen, Doyle, don't go spreading the word about Manuel around. I'll have every housewife from Boca to Port St. Lucie calling me."

Doyle exhales heavily. "Why am I so exhausted?"

"It's been a long time coming. It took a lot of planning, but you pulled it off."

"What's next?" Doyle sips her champagne.

"You go home, take off your heels and relax." Kim smiles. "Before you know it, you'll be planning your next one."

"Oh, don't you dare say that. I'm never doing this again."

Kim pats Doyle's shoulder. "Oh sweetie, in ten years he'll be turning sixty and you'll have to do this again."

Kim laughs as she grabs the string of a balloon and hands it to Doyle. Doyle bats it away with her hand.

4

THE DREAM CATCHER

"Are you ready?" Jen asked.

"No," Lenora answered.

"When are you going to be ready?" Jen felt Lenora's hand tremble in hers.

"Never." Lenora leaned forward and looked over the edge. The water below was clear and still. She could see the rocks lining the bottom of the mountain lake. "I don't think it's deep enough."

"We were just swimming down there. You saw, it's at least twenty feet deep."

"Yeah, but we're so high up here." Lenora stared across the horizon. They had only climbed thirty feet from the base to the cliff. She looked back to where she thought their campsite was.

She traced the highway as it wound through stands of pine trees until it was eclipsed by the intersecting branches.

"You just saw those guys do it." Jen pointed over her shoulder at the two dripping teenage boys standing behind them.

The blonde boy spoke up, "Can we sneak past you while you think it over?"

The other boy, plump and tan, tried to reassure Lenora. "It's so much fun."

Lenora carefully moved away from the edge and waved the boys past. The blonde one ran and sprung from the edge. He did two front flips and then slowed his rotation so that his feet broke the water before he slipped below the surface with barely a splash.

"He's showing off. I think he likes you," the tan one said to Jen. She watched as the blonde boy swam a backstroke to the shore.

"All right, look out," the tan boy demanded. He took three steps back and then ran for the edge. He sprung into the clear with his arms spread. He tilted forward and pierced the surface, making even less of a splash than the blonde boy.

The girls watched him as he swam to the shore to meet his friend. The boys made their way back to the path to climb up to the ledge again.

Jen's father, Harold Crenshaw, was sitting on the blanket he had thrown over the fine gravel beach. Her mother, Renee, lie on the blanket next to him. Jesse, her younger brother, skipped rocks further down the shore.

Harold waved from down below. Jen and Lenora waved back. Now that he had their attention, Harold pointed to the watch on his arm. Renee rubbed her belly.

"Time for lunch. It's now or never, Ra Ra." Jen crouched a little as if to ready herself to start for the edge. She reached out for Lenora's hand but her grip slipped away. "Ewww, gross." Jen frowned at her hand.

"Sorry. I'm nervous." Lenora wiped her hands together.

"I guess so." Jen wiped her palm on the back of her suit. "Come on, before those boys get back." She reached out again.

"Maybe we should wait for them. I think the blonde one really does like you."

Jen's face turned pink. "Oh jeez, really?"

"That's what the chubby one said."

"I thought he was just teasing me."

They could hear the boys' shouts as they neared. Jen summoned her courage. She turned and ran off the edge. She fell to the water below, her body in the shape of an L. The back of her legs smacked against the surface.

Crack

Jen lay on her belly on the beach blanket as her mother and Lenora rubbed ice up and down the back of her red thighs. Jen held her face in her hands. The two boys stood a few feet off. The tan boy held his hand over his mouth to hide his smile and snickers.

"I didn't see it but, boy, did I hear it," the blonde one said.

"Thank you, young man. What's your name?" Harold asked, walking toward him with his hand extended.

"I'm Zach." He grabbed Harold's hand and squeezed it tight.

"You're a strong swimmer," Harold said and then pointed towards his daughter. "I was about to jump in there but you were right on it."

"We swim a lot, Adam and me," Zach said and pointed his thumb at his friend.

"Are you boys on the team at school?"

"This is my school." Adam gestured around at the trees lining the mountain lake.

"Adam lives on the Indian lands, just north of Keystone. I don't think they have a swim team there." Zach spoke for his friend. "I live over by Rockerville."

Young Jesse stood close behind his father and peered at the boys. He was a shy but curious boy.

"Come here, Jesse." Harold pulled his son around by the hand. "This is Zach. He helped your sister when she was hurt just now."

"Nice to meet you, Jesse." Zach smiled down at the boy. "Did you know there was a famous guy named Jesse that once made his way around these parts?"

"Jesse James?" The boy looked at his father to see if he was correct. Harold pointed to Zach.

"That's right. In fact, there's a place back east toward Sioux City called Devil's Gulch. Jesse James jumped clear over it one time trying to get away from the sheriff."

Jesse's eyes lit and he looked to his father for confirmation. "Zach's right, Jesse. You know, we could check that out on the drive back home. Would you like that?"

Jesse nodded.

"Tell me, Adam, what is it like to grow up on Native American land?" Harold asked.

Adam shook his head no. "We are not called Native Americans. You should call us Indians or First People."

"Oh my God, Dad!?" Jen shot arrows from her eyes. Renee and Lenora stopped icing Jen's legs to see how Harold would respond.

"Please pardon me." Harold shrunk and grimaced. "I'm actually a history teacher. I should have known better."

Adam stepped forward. He was barely a teenager but carried himself solemnly, like an old soul. "It's not your fault. Your history books are backwards. Take that park where that battle happened." He pointed down the highway. "When the Americans invade and they lose, it's called a slaughter and they build a memorial. When the Americans win, they say they put down the insurrection and they build a monument."

Harold frowned. "I'd love to chat and learn more."

"Dad!" Jen brought herself to her feet with a groan. "Leave him alone."

"Let me buy you guys lunch," Harold said to the boys while looking at Jen. She hesitated and looked to Lenora, who nodded her approval.

"I have to work this afternoon." Adam shrugged.

Zach smiled at Jen and she smiled back. "I'd like to go to lunch," he said.

"Do you boys need a ride?" Renee asked as she rose to her feet and dusted off her legs.

"No, ma'am. We have our bikes over by those trees over there." Zach pointed.

Suddenly, a dull thunder grabbed their attention. Lenora and the Crenshaws looked around at the clear sky, trying to locate the rumble. The sound reverberated through the rocks and the trees, making it impossible to pinpoint. Jesse ran to his mother and grabbed her leg. She pet his crop of brown hair as she peered into the distance.

"I think we're about to get a storm," Renee said.

"No, ma'am." Zach smiled.

The thunder didn't fade. It grew in volume and what at first sounded like random spasms took on a rhythm. It sounded like a train engine in the distance, then grew as though someone was dialing up an amplifier ever so slowly. They knew it was coming from the west now. They all looked down the highway in anticipation.

Jesse clung so tight to his mother's shorts that he began to pull them down. Renee grabbed at her waistband and yanked them back up.

Jen looked at Zach. Her face spelled wonder and anticipation. His did, too.

The first two bikers appeared from around the corner, riding double-file. Another pair trailed right behind them and another after them. Jesse crouched behind his mother as the first of them passed, but crept out for a closer look as fascination overwhelmed his fear. A parade of black leather-clad cowboys astride metal horses, pistons pounding and carburetors belching as they tore down the mountain highway.

One biker caught sight of Jesse and waved to him. Jesse waved back excitedly and ran closer to the highway. He thrust his arm above his head and swung the whole thing from shoulder to fingertips. Every biker after that waved back. One saluted.

When the last pair of cycles passed, Jesse trotted down after them, still waving. Finally, the din passed and the serene silence of the mountain landscape reclaimed their senses.

The boys had retrieved their bikes while Lenora and the Crenshaw family watched the passing biker gang. The boys sat in their saddles with their arms at their sides.

"Cool," Lenora whispered when she noticed them. "I thought they meant bicycles."

Jesse saw them and ran to Zach's thigh. Zach picked him up and sat him across the gas tank. The child reached for the handlebars and tried to turn them.

Renee looked at Zach as he held her son on his dirt bike. "How old are you boys?"

Adam kick-started his dirt bike and shouted, "Old enough to ride!"

Jesse stared at the machine with fascination, while holding his palms firmly over his ears. The small engine on the bike whined and revved like a broken blender. The contrast in tone from the passing choppers was stark. Adam twisted the throttle and made his way to the edge of the highway. Zach waited back.

Zach picked up Jesse and placed him off to the side. He looked directly at Jen. "Come meet us for lunch at Adam's family's place," he said. "They've got good food."

Jen looked to her father. He nodded and answered, "OK, should we follow you?"

Zach chuckled. "No, sir. You'd never make it down the roads we'll be taking. Just follow 16 east until you get to Hill City. The place is called the Dream Catcher Restaurant and Casino."

Zach jumped and kicked his right heel back like a mule. The dirt bike screamed to life. Jesse jumped backed and grabbed his mom's leg, then he smiled and bounced in approval. Zach slowly brought the bike up to the roadside next to Adam. He waved one last time and then they crossed the highway and disappeared down the other side. The bikes revved and two clouds of dust peeked over the edge of the highway. Jesse clapped his hands all along until the last whine of the 150cc motors faded in the distance.

"Are you familiar with the three blessings, Mr. Crenshaw?" the woman asked Harold as she placed a French fry in her mouth. Her name was Shoanna. She had brown skin and long black hair. She wore layers of jewelry on her ears, neck, wrists, and fingers. The trinkets and baubles clanged and rattled with every movement.

Ting

Tang

Ting

"Yes, the ancient Hebrews would thank God that they were born free, born as men and born Jewish. Well, a subset of them would I suppose." Harold laughed nervously. He took a sip of his soda and set the red plastic cup down on the picnic table.

The Dream Catcher Restaurant and Casino was a gas station with a small complex of businesses attached. There was a convenience store in front, which is where the Crenshaws found Adam manning the register. There were western-style swinging doors in the back, and beyond them was the gift shop. It was packed with souvenirs. There were collectible magnets, spoons, mugs and hats. T-shirts emblazoned with pictures of Sitting Bull, Mount Rushmore, and assorted woodland creatures hung on the walls. Dream catchers, which are hoops with woven patterns, hung from the ceiling everywhere. The hang tag of one explained that dream catchers are intended to protect children from danger as they slept, while also capturing their fondest dreams.

Through yet another set of swinging doors was the largest room. A large box with a high vaulted ceiling, the room seemed like an enormous steel barn. On the left side was a long bar with a constellation of electric beer signs beaming. On the right side was a lunch counter serving burgers, hot dogs and other concession stand food. Lining the back wall were electronic gambling machines that whistled and beeped and blinked and beckoned the patrons sitting at the picnic tables spread across the concrete floor.

Shoanna set her cup down. "Hmm, I never knew the blessings started with the Hebrews. Our version is a little different. Very different actually."

"Please tell me about your version." Harold folded his hands in front of himself.

"The Lakota thank God for family, community and the forest." Shoanna reached out and patted Harold's folded hands. "If you want to learn about the Lakota, that's where to start. Everything starts with our family."

"Do you have rituals?"

"We have schools and churches on our land, just like you."

"I see, what about the nature part?"

"We leave it alone. And we protect it."

Harold looked up and nodded his head. "Of course, of course."

While Shoanna and Harold talked, Renee and Lenora busied themselves with the music on the jukebox. Knowing that her husband would be spending some time talking to Shoanna, Renee fed five dollars into the machine. That bought them thirty songs, but they still made their selections judiciously.

Jen sat with Zach, and so did Jesse. The boy was holstered on Zach's hip.

"Thanks for indulging my dad," Jen told him.

"Thanks for coming out here for lunch." Zack grabbed Jesse around the shoulder and gave him a squeeze. "Shoanna loves to talk about their culture. Adam loves her. That's where he learns all that stuff about his history."

"Is she his mommy?" Jesse asked.

"That's his aunt, his mommy's sister," Zach told him.

"She's pretty," Jesse said.

"She is pretty," Jen agreed.

"You better tell your mom to watch out." Zach laughed and grabbed a fry from his basket.

Jen gazed at Zach, oblivious to her parents. He caught her stare and fixed his eyes to hers, while still chewing. He swallowed and wiped his mouth with his napkin.

"I think you're pretty," he told Jen.

Jesse wiggled away from Zach and giggled.

Jen ignored her brother. Her stare stayed with his. "Me, too."

Zach laughed.

"Oh, jeez." Jen moaned, her face falling to her palms. "I meant . . . oh, jeez . . . I meant . . . likewise."

Zach laughed harder, then he stood up and held out his hand. "Come on, there's a dirt track out back. Let me show you."

Jen popped up from her seat and took his hand. They floated to the door with Jesse skipping behind. Jen caught sight of

Lenora, who gave a quick tip of her head in approval. Her mother waved. "Jesse, over here, sweetie. Let your sister visit with her new friend."

Jesse turned and pouted, but then he saw some of the black-leather cowboys sitting at the table near his father. They looked just like the men he saw on the motorcycles by the lake, except now he could make out every detail of their garb: chains hanging from their back pockets, leather vests with flaming skulls on the back, and patches stitched all over. There were eight-ball patches, and ace-of-spades patches, and lightning patches, and heart patches.

Jesse ran to his father, who was in rapt conversation with Shoanna. Jesse looked at his mother; she and Lenora were concentrating on the jukebox. With no one paying attention to him, he wandered out the door to follow Jen and Zach.

Jen stood with her arms folded on the top row of the bleachers next to the track. Zach ripped around the far turn to the left. He turned straight for the stretch. His motor screamed and buzzed like a hundred chainsaws cutting at once. He approached a large mound in the track and Jen raised her hands to cover her eyes but stopped short.

Zach hit the jump and shot into the air. He reached such a height that Jen had to crane her neck to watch him. She placed both hands over her mouth. As Zach reached the apex of his jump, he kicked his legs out behind himself and reached back with his left hand. He looked like Superman. He repositioned himself in the saddle before landing on the track below. Jen brought her hands to her heart in prayer. Zach made another turn and hit the next jumps in the track. Jen's head bobbed up and down as Zach bounced around the course like a rubber ball.

He made his way down the stretch again and made his big jump. In mid-air, Zach shot both legs out to the left and then to the right, like a gymnast on a pommel horse. Instead of praying, Jen clapped. He tore around the track again and again, each time showing off a new trick when he reached the largest jump.

Jen bounced on the balls of her feet the next time he reached the far turn. She looked at the large mound in anticipation. Then she saw Jesse, lying prone in the grass right at the edge of the track. He was resting his chin in his hands, looking up at the jump.

"Jesse!" she screamed. "You can't be there!"

Jesse could not hear her over the whine of Zach's engine.

"Jesse, move!" Jen screamed again. She jumped and waved her arms.

Zach noticed Jen's panicked gestures. Distracted, he hit the peak of the jump at an angle and the tail end of the bike whipped out from beneath him. With his right leg, he reached out to grab the saddle of the machine with his heel. He brought the bike true only to see Jesse staring straight up at him.

"Jesseeeeee!" Jen screamed. Jesse was transfixed by the heavy motor bike about to crush him.

Zach took his legs from around the bike and pushed it away from himself, toward the infield. The screaming ceased as he released the handlebars and the throttle snapped shut. The bike landed with a crash and skipped on the track, throwing up clouds of dirt and oily black smoke along the way. Zach hit the ground with a reverberating thud. He writhed in the dirt but made no sound. Jesse stood and stared at him from the edge of the track. He had never moved from his spot. Jen ran to Zach. She struggled to get his helmet off. Zach moaned and grunted, like a caveman.

"He just has the wind knocked out of him," Adam shouted. He was striding down the track toward them, along with a crowd of folks from the bar, including Renee and Lenora.

"It sounds like he's dying." Jen was crying now. She held her right hand in a fist and bit on her knuckle.

"I've seen him much worse than this." Adam reached beneath Zach's armpits and sat him upright. With his weight behind Zach, he took Zack's arms and stretched them out in front of him and then to the side. Adam repeated the action and finally Zach's lungs expanded to take in a breath.

GASP

Zach lunged forward with his mouth agape. He looked like he had just surfaced from a deep dive. Jen approached, but Adam held her off with an outstretched arm. Jen turned and saw her little brother, still standing at the edge of the track, looking sheepish.

Jen's face twisted into a ferocious scowl. "You little shit," she seethed. "Do you see what you did? You almost killed him!"

Jen ran toward Jesse with her arm raised. Jesse flinched and curled up to protect himself. Renee intercepted her daughter before she could harm him.

"Jennifer Ray!" Renee took her daughter by her shoulders. "You need to get a hold of yourself."

"You didn't see what he did." Jen looked past her mother and pointed at Jesse.

"I'll take care of it." Renee pushed Jen back and pointed back to the bar. "Go find your father. He needs your help."

Jen looked over and saw Zach retrieving his bike. He propped it up and Adam knelt to assess the damage.

Lenora walked next to Jen and put her arm around her. "Come on, Jen, you should go see your dad."

Jen asked, "What's his problem now?"

Lenora began to answer but found herself snickering instead.

"What? What is it?" Jen shook her head.

Lenora paused, looked at Jen and then laughed even harder. "He wants to go on a vision quest," she finally answered.

Harold sat at the bar with a bucket on the barstool next to him. The bikers were filing out through the gift shop door. The last of them turned and waved back. "Happy trails, Harold."

The bartender, a stocky Indian, looked at the man and growled, "I told you to get the fuck out of here." Noticing Jen and Lenora approaching, he said, "Pardon me, ladies, but those men did something most uncourteous to your father."

"What did they do?" Jen bolted to her dad.

Harold looked at his daughter and his face lit with affection. "Darling, you're here."

Jen looked over her shoulder and then back to her dad. "I wasn't gone that long. What happened to you?"

Shoanna was mopping the floor beneath the picnic table where they had been talking. "One of the Desert Aces thought it would be cute to slip some shrooms on your dad's burger."

"I'm on a vision quest!" Harold shouted. A red bucket sat on the stool at his side.

"Drink this." The bartender slid a glass in front of Harold.

"What's he giving him?" Jen demanded.

"That's my husband, Joseph," Shoanna assured her. "He's giving him sugar water."

Joseph told her, "It'll soothe his stomach."

"Look at this wood knot right here." Harold pointed at the bar top. "Veins of oak are passing around it like streams of water. There's something written in it."

Lenora indulged him. "What's it say, Mr. Crenshaw?"

Harold peered at the graffiti. He looked so closely that his nose almost touched the bar. He brought his head back, rubbed his eyes and then brought his face back as close as it was before.

"Mr. Crenshaw?"

Harold popped up and looked at Lenora. "It says, 'You only live once. Jeff. Eight, one, ninety-nine.'"

Lenora nodded and looked at Jen with an amused grin. Jen shook her head and looked at Shoanna.

Shoanna wrung out the mop into the bucket. "Hope you don't have any plans for the next couple hours."

"Jeff, eight one, ninety-nine," Harold repeated. He looked at Joseph. "Why did Jeff eat one ninety-nine? What is that even?"

"Ninety-nine is odd," Joseph toyed with Harold, but wiped away his smile when he saw Jen. "He's going to be fine. He'll probably have a great time. But Shoanna's right, you probably should hang around here for a while. Don't worry, I'll take care of him."

Zach walked slowly through the open doors. He held his ribs on his right side as though to keep them from popping out. "How's it going in here?"

"Mr. Crenshaw's on a vision quest," Lenora blurted.

"I heard," Zach said as Adam trailed behind him, chatting with Renee and Jesse.

Harold saw Zach. "Young man, why did Jeff eat ninety-nine?"

Adam looked back at his uncle Joseph. "Holy shit, he's really trippin'."

Zach began to laugh but then groaned and grabbed his side with both hands.

Jen gazed at Zach. "Are you okay?"

"I'll be fine. Just a couple ribs." Zach slapped himself on his uninjured side. "I've got more."

The song playing on the jukebox ended. When another song didn't start playing, Lenora looked at Renee. "Was that the last one?"

Joseph stuck his hand in his tip jar and pulled out a five. "Adam, how about you play a nice little soundtrack for Harold's vision quest. Keep it calm and relaxing, please."

"Can I help you?" Lenora asked Adam. He shrugged and waved her to the jukebox.

Harold walked the length of the bar, looking for more messages. His nose was but an inch from the surface, and his right index finger traced the wood grain. "I found another one."

"What's it say?" Joseph asked.

"Sturgis, ninety-eight. Mitch and Logan."

"Are you sure we should be walking this far?" Jen looked back down the path toward the Dream Catcher. She could see the roof of the building.

"Are you scared?" Zach turned to face her.

"I mean, how much higher are we going?"

"You think this is high?" Zach started walking again. "I ride my bike up here all the time."

"I don't doubt it." Jen stared up the corridor cutting through the forest of spruce trees. The branches started high up the trunk and they made a ceiling as they stretched over the path. "Where are we going again?"

Zach stopped and waved her closer. As she approached, he slipped his arm around her waist and squeezed her body close to his left side. Zach craned his neck and bowed his head toward her. With his right hand, he pointed between the tops of trees. "There, up there, see that ledge?"

Jen ignored whatever it was he pointed at. She was fixated on this boy's embrace and his face so close to hers. She reached behind him and wrapped her arm around his right side. She squeezed.

"Owwwwwww!" Zach jerked away and howled in pain.

"Oh my God. I'm so sorry."

Zach guarded his right side with his arm. "Come on."

"I'm so sorry," Jen said again, crouching with one hand to her mouth and the other reaching out to Zach. "I'm so sorry."

Zach gathered himself. "It's no big deal. It just hurts, you know?"

"Of course, I was there."

Zach reached out a hand and interlaced his fingers with hers. They walked up the path. He pointed out a bird. "Yellow rumped warbler."

"I'm sorry?"

"Yellow rumped warbler." He pointed at a tiny bird perched on the branch of a fir tree.

"Neat." Jen smiled and pointed across the path. "How about that one?"

"Dark eyed junco."

"Well that sounds made up."

"I swear," Zach said, placing his hand on his heart. "It's a dark eyed junco."

"How do you know all this?" Jen started walking again and pulled him along.

"Adam knows every bird and bug in these hills. He taught me everything."

"Ah, so Adam gets the credit." Jen nodded.

They chatted as they strolled up the path until it got steeper and rockier. The ledge was close now, but they had several boulders to negotiate before getting there. The path was uneven and full of rocks, so they went single file with Zach leading the way. Jen watched each footfall as she carefully walked the path.

Zach reached the ledge first but he turned and waited for Jen before climbing up. He reached out his hand and pulled her close once she caught up. She was out of breath and some of her bangs clung to the sweat on her forehead.

"Now what?" she asked him.

"I'm going to give you a boost to that perch there and then you just climb up onto the ledge." Zach interlaced his fingers and leaned over to make a stirrup for Jen to step into. She followed his queue and he hoisted her onto the perch. Zach climbed up on his own, wincing and moaning as he did so. They climbed up to the ledge together and stood with their hands on their waists.

Jen breathed heavily as she took in the view. Rows of fir trees stood like fuzzy green pencils carpeting the jagged hills laid out before her. "Wow. It's breathtaking." She noticed the restaurant far down below. She turned to Zach and asked, "Why is it called the Dream Catcher?"

Zach guarded his right side with his right arm and reached out to Jen with his left. She reached out and let him draw her closer. He wrapped his arm around her back and kissed her softly on the lips.

5

NAPLES (NOT FLORIDA)

Hello, my name is Chris Carlisle and I was in a riot. I didn't expect to be in a riot and I certainly did nothing to start it. Hell, you couldn't even call it a riot until the cops showed up and started whoopin' ass. Sure, the crowd was chanting, and they lit a couple fires, but it was chilly, after all. I was walking to the train station, taking it all in and then the cops started clubbing the scrapple out of people. When it's all said and done, I enjoyed it. Granted, I may not have had the same opinion if I had my head split by a baton but, overall, it was a blast. I'd definitely do it again.

It was March of 2003. I was touring with a punk band called The Extra Medium. We were on a winter circuit around Europe with a bunch of other bands. We started in Scandinavia on the first of the year because that's when it would be the coldest and the darkest. You know, the most punk thing we could do.

We ended the tour in Naples in mid-March. That's the Naples in Italy, not the one in Florida, obviously. In any case, Naples is pure, fucking chaos. The punk scene could have been born there. The whole place is nothing but dark, dirty alleys covered in graffiti. I know that sounds like any city you've ever been, but in Naples the alleys are teeming with life. You take a turn down any of them and there's people drinking and smoking and selling shit. And when I say they're selling shit, I don't just mean dope. There are, like, bakeries and shoe stores and stuff. These alleys are where the people live and do their daily business.

We had just finished two nights of shows around town and had to catch the 5:40 pm train to Rome. We would have driven but the rental agency wouldn't let us take a car into Naples. The only guy who managed to score a vehicle was our manager, Nick Bridgeway. He had lied and managed to rent a van in Rome. It was loaded with all of our gear, so we had to train it from there to Naples. He was going to drive it back up to Rome, where we'd meet him and then take a flight back to DC.

I handed my bag to Nick and started to jog away.

"Where you going?" Nick asked as he threw my stuff in the van.

"I promised my mother a rosary from Italy."

"Dude, we're going back to Rome in less than an hour." Our bassist, Kit, tried to reason with me.

"I want one with those little red horns on it," I told him. "I just saw one back there. I'll catch up with you on the platform."

I turned to trot away, but my buddy Ricky waved me over. "Is it far?" he asked.

"Nah, right down that alley over there. You want to come?"

Ricky was in this band out of Chicago called the Sport Peppers. They usually followed us in the lineup, and we had gotten to know each other during the tour. They had more shows scheduled so they weren't heading back yet. "Yeah, I need to kill some time," he said.

Ricky and I hustled off the concrete apron outside the massive vestibule of the station.

"See you in DC, dipshit!" Kit yelled after me.

We made it to the street but I couldn't find the shop.

"You lost?" Ricky smirked.

"No, I know it's around here."

"I think you're lost."

I stopped and turned. "Fuck off then."

"I'm just saying, man, all these dumps look the same. It's easy to mistake one for the next."

He wasn't wrong there. The problem was that there were a bunch of places that had closed their steel shutters around five and others that had just opened up. I had lost all my points of reference.

"There was a mechanic right here." I pointed at a place with a steel door rolled down across the front. The sign above it said Idraulico. "See? Idraulico the mechanic."

"That means plumber." Ricky shook his head.

"How the hell do you know?" I searched the sign looking for any word that resembled mechanic so I could prove him wrong.

"I'm Italian."

"I thought your last name was Baker?" I continued walking down the street and away from the station. A nasty stray dog scurried across the street. Her swollen teats swung pendulously below her belly. Three black pups trailed after her.

"Mother's side. Her maiden name's Schiavo."

"Oh yeah, what's Schiavo mean?"

"Slave."

We walked another block down. There was a government building that took up an entire city block. The foundation stones were as big as box trucks. They were like canvasses for the street artists. The graffiti stretched on and on like a gigantic, continuous mural.

"We've gone too far. I remember this one." A painting of Fidel Castro alongside Che Guevara graced the wall. The two portraits were both taller than a grown man, each wider than one could reach their arms across. Something was written next to the painting.

"What's that say, Ricky?"

"It's pretty fucking boss, actually," Ricky said and nodded his approval. "It says: Class against class, until victory. The enemy is the boss. The fascist is the speculator, not those with different colored skin."

"Yeah, that's pretty badass," I agreed. I kept looking for the jewelry shop.

"Yo, Chris. It's like ten after, you know?"

I put my hands on my hips and looked up and down the street, hoping to see something familiar. "Oh well, I'll just get her one in Rome."

"I mean, yeah man, it's friggin' Rome. You can get her a rosary and a statue of Mary at the airport."

"I really liked the one with the horns though." I started walking back toward the station. "You know, those little red horns they have around here? They made up all the beads on the necklace. It was dope."

"You mean like that?" Ricky pointed in the window of a store. The rosary I was looking for was in the showcase.

"What the hell? This is it." I looked up and down the storefront. "We walked right past it."

Ricky tapped the face of his watch. "All right man, you better get in there."

An old man and woman sat behind the counter. They didn't move an inch or offer any greeting.

"Do you speak English?" I looked back and forth at their faces. They stared at me. The man smiled.

"I want to buy something, this rosary over here." I turned and tapped my finger on the glass of the showcase that held the item.

They stared at me. The woman smiled.

I rushed outside. "Ricky, I'm going to need your help."

Ricky flicked his smoke to the ground and sauntered into the store in front of me.

"Salve, buona sera." He waved to the couple.

They rose to their feet, smiled and began yammering in Italian.

"All right, tell them it's this one over here." I tapped on the glass again.

Ricky raised his palm to me and kept talking to the couple. They seemed intrigued by whatever he had to say.

"What are they saying?"

He raised his palm to me again.

What could I do? I waited. I looked around the store. I realized it wasn't exactly a jewelry store and definitely not just a souvenir shop. One showcase was full of war medals. There were a bunch of Italian medals and many from other countries, too. I noticed an Iron Cross from Germany and something that looked to be French, based on the colors. There was even an American Purple Heart that snuck in there somehow.

Another showcase held vintage sunglasses. Another had old watches, small clocks and other devices like barometers and compasses. I looked up at the wall behind this counter and there were framed maps and old banners. The banners must have had something to do with soccer teams, I guess. On the shelf below the maps and banners were trophies and lamps. I turned to the right and looked at the showcase at the back of the store. There were coins, corroded utensils and old porcelain plates and cups.

There was more history in just one corner of this shitty little shop than I had bothered to see during my three month tour of Europe.

The conversation between the old couple and Ricky stopped. Ricky turned to me. "How much?"

"What?"

"How much do you want to pay for the rosary?" Ricky asked.

"Aren't they supposed to tell me?"

"That's not how it works here."

I looked at the showcase of coins and kitchenware and noticed there were no prices listed. I looked at the banners and maps; didn't look to be any tags on them either. I shrugged and raised my hands. "I dunno, ten euro?"

The couple erupted into hysterics, shouting and making wild gesticulations. The man brought his hand to his face, placed his fingers beneath his chin and flung them forward like he was flicking a crop of whiskers at me. The woman brought her hand to her face, bared her teeth and then bounced her index finger off her top bridge. Then, in unison, they slapped their inner elbows as they shot their forearms into the air.

"They are upset with you," Ricky told me.

"I gathered that."

Ricky spoke with them in Italian and they seemed to calm down.

"What did you tell them?"

"I told them the truth. That this is a gift for your mother and that you could have bought one in Rome, but you insisted on buying this one here."

"Can you tell them we are in a hurry, too?"

"I did."

"OK, so how much is it?" I threw my hands in the air.

I do not know what Ricky said next but we clearly were not negotiating from a position of strength. He turned to me. "Eighty American dollars."

"Get the fuck out of here." I waved him off.

The man rose and started pointing at the showcase that held the piece. He was earnest but not as angry as before.

Ricky listened, then nodded with appreciation.

"Well?" I asked.

"That was the rosary of the great-great-granddaughter of King Carlo himself."

"And I'm my great-uncle's favorite niece," I replied. "Who gives a fuck?"

There was silence. I looked at my watch. It was 5:30.

"I have to run. Tell them I said thanks anyway."

Before Ricky could tell him, the old man said his first words in English. "Fifty bucks, American."

"Son of a . . ." I muttered but Ricky cut me off.

"He'll take it," Ricky told the man.

"I'm not paying fifty for that." I scoffed. "And what's wrong with euro?"

"I want dollars," the man shrugged.

I looked in my wallet. "The only dollars I have are two twenties and I need those for a cab in DC."

"Come on, man. Bridgeway will take care of you when you land," Ricky said.

I glared at Ricky. "I didn't want to spend more than twenty." I looked at my watch again.

"OK, forty dollars." The old man went to the showcase before I could answer. His wife placed a blue felt mat atop the glass showcase.

I narrowed my eyes and held my stare on the old man. "I thought you didn't speak English."

"I never said that," he said with a smile. "My name is Angelo. This is my wife, Lucia."

Angelo set the piece atop the blue felt and Lucia set to straightening it out and dabbing it with a white cloth. It was pretty. The silver of the metal chain glistened.

"Hey, Chris, you really need to hustle. What do you want to do?" Ricky looked anxiously about.

"Fine, fine." I reached in my wallet and handed the cash to Angelo. He nodded appreciation and then sent Lucia away with the piece.

"Wait, where is she going?" I asked.

"You said it was a gift," Angelo replied.

"Sir, I don't have time for this." I watched him secure my cash in his back pocket.

"It won't take but a moment."

I looked at Ricky. He shrugged.

"I got like five minutes."

Lucia arrived from the back with a small, ornate box. It was fire red, just like the horns on the rosary. She pulled a length of ribbon from a spool and cut it. The ribbon was wide and of a heavy gauge. It was a deep, dark orange. She wrapped the ribbon around the box carefully and then tied it off in a perfect bow.

She handed the box to me with both hands and bowed a little as she did so. "A beautiful gift from a son to his mother."

The moment captured me. I was happy that I spent forty dollars. "Thank you, Lucia. Thank you, Angelo."

"Dude." Ricky nodded toward the door.

I instantly regretted even that small hesitation. We bolted out the door.

"Arrivederci!" I heard the couple shout as we hit the street.

At this point, you might be expecting details of a mad dash through the street with me bumping into people, dodging cars and tripping on the sidewalk. To be sure, all of those things did happen, and yes, I still missed my train, but as I told you at the outset, that's not what makes this story interesting.

I stood on the platform clutching the red box in both hands. Ricky strolled up the platform smoking a cigarette.

"Sorry, brother." He flicked his smoke on the tracks where my train had sat a moment earlier. "The amazing thing here is that a train out of Naples actually left on time."

"Fuck."

"Come on, let's see when the next train leaves." Ricky gave me a pat. "You'll be fine. You'll catch up with them tonight."

We walked back inside and found the board. The next train to Rome was at 9:40. I went to the window and exchanged my ticket.

"Thanks for sticking around." We walked out of the station with Piazza Garibaldi before us. "You want to get some pizza?"

Ricky ignored me. Something else caught his attention. "What's all this then?"

There was a huge crowd of people gathered at the far side of the piazza. A boulevard ran west from the station. It split the piazza down the middle and ended where it made a T with Corso Garibaldi, which ran north and south. The crowd, it was still a crowd and not yet a mob, looked to be concentrated there.

"You want to check this out?" he asked.

"Hell yeah."

The piazza was several blocks wide from north to south and even wider from east to west. We spent a few minutes walking before we began to hear the murmur of the crowd and feel the buzz of their energy.

"Oh shit, I bet this is a war protest," Ricky said.

"Did we invade?"

"They said we were about to. I'm not sure."

"What do they care?" As we walked closer, I looked at the signs they were holding. One had American and British flags dripping in blood. I saw one with Bush with devil horns. He held missiles in each hand as he rode atop a bomber. I saw another with Uncle Sam as a puppeteer. One of the puppets he held on his strings was Tony Blair but there were two others I didn't recognize. I pointed and asked Ricky, "Who are those guys?"

"The one on the left is Tony Blair and the guy on the right is Silvio Berlusconi. I'm not sure about the other." He looked around and found another Berlusconi. He pointed and then found another one and pointed with his free hand. "Italy must have joined the coalition, too. That's what they're so pissed about."

We mingled with the crowd. Ricky asked people what was going on. The U.S. had invaded, and the people were indeed pissed. He whispered, "Some of them just want to wreck shit. Fuckin' anarchists."

"I love it."

"Most of them are pissed about Berlusconi though." He kept his American voice low. "They say shit's going to get real after dinner."

"Why after dinner?"

"They're Italians. Dinner comes first. This is just staging."

"Staging?"

"It looks like a mess but they're actually planning. There are different factions here. They're all telling each other where they are planning to go and when." He pointed to the red banners. "Those are the Commies; they're going to city hall. Over there in black are the neofascists, they're going to the Piazza of the Plebiscite. We better hope they keep their distance."

"They're like oil and water, huh?"

"More like sparks and black powder."

"Wow." I squeezed the gift box tight in my hands. "This is awesome."

We started meeting people in the crowd. They were like benevolent psychopaths. I started to feel at home. I wanted to learn Italian. I wanted to return to Naples and I hadn't even left yet.

We got the scoop on when things would go down. They told us how everyone would disperse to separate parts of the city so that the cops would have to spread themselves out. They all agreed to meet back at Corso Garibaldi at 9:00 pm.

"You want to go get that pizza now?" I asked Ricky. "We got some time before the show."

"Oh shit, that's right. You got a show tonight. What time?"

"We need to set up around nine."

"Damn." I frowned. Ricky had proved to be quite helpful. "Come on, let's walk down to the waterfront and find some beers."

We walked south down Corso Garibaldi until we reached the seafront promenade. The lamps lining the seafront cast an orange-yellow light that contrasted sharply with the red Christmas lights adorning a vendor's wagon. As I got closer, I realized that the lights were shaped like the same little red horns comprising the rosary nested in the little box I carried under my arm.

"This town is as beautiful as it is ugly." I looked down the promenade, past the sailboats in the harbor to the lights of the homes on the periphery of the city. The homes scaled up the slopes of Vesuvius for a good part of the way and then stopped just like a tree line on a mountain.

As we approached the man tending the vendor's wagon, he handed both of us a little pastry.

"Grazie mille," Ricky told the guy and then turned to me. "It's called a baba'. It's soaked in rum."

I popped it in my mouth. It was a sweet little sponge with an after-kick. I shook my head in amazement. "This town is as friendly as it is dangerous."

Ricky ordered two beers from the man and I paid him. We walked down the promenade in silence for a while. There was the sea to our left and grand hotels to our right. The hotels had massive archways framing the front windows and massive marquees above the front entrances. The folks in the top floors must have had an amazing view of the sea and the castle that was plopped right down in the middle of the harbor.

"That's Ovo's castle," Ricky said, pointing. "There's a magic egg in the foundation, if you believe Virgil."

"Who the fuck is Virgil?"

"The ancient poet, Virgil." Ricky looked at me like I was the one talking nonsense.

"Hmm?"

"They never made you read the classics in high school? Homer, Virgil?"

"I know Homer Simpson and Virgil the wrestler," I joked and sipped my beer. "Dude, I barely finished high school."

The wrought-iron railing that ran along the promenade led us to the jetty then to the fortified castle. The stone walls were forty feet high. The building was square and squat; a stocky, impenetrable cube, surrounded by restaurants and souvenir shops.

There were mostly seafood places, but we found a pizza joint and grabbed a table.

We ordered a couple more beers before looking at the menu, then we watched a local hustler shake down tourists. He was trying to get them to buy tickets to enter the castle. The castle was clearly closed.

"For domani. . . for tomorrow, tomorrow morning. Castle open at eight," the man assured the tourists in broken English.

I pointed the top of my beer bottle at the crooked man. "I like this. I find it reassuring."

Ricky nodded. "I know, it's like wherever you go in the world, you find the same idiocy."

"The world is just one big city. You find the same kind of crazies wherever you go." I placed my hand on the gift box to make sure it was still there on the table.

A man came striding up the jetty at that moment. He was pointing at the scalper and he marched toward him. A woman trailed behind him at a much slower pace.

"You! You're a liar!" He shouted in English. He had only a slight accent. I guessed he was German. He turned and shouted to anyone who would listen, "Do not buy tickets from this man!"

The scalper pointed to himself and made a convincing "Who me?" face. He shook his head no and waved his arms at the man. The marks he was working on scurried away.

When the German was within arm's reach of the scalper, he produced two tickets from his back pocket and waved them in the hustler's face. "These tickets were good for YESTERDAY!" He shouted and smacked the tickets with his free hand. The man's companion kept a slight distance.

The Napolitano was short, much shorter than the lean German. The scalper was stocky like a pug, so it wasn't a total mismatch, but the German definitely had him on reach.

"Give me my money back." The German thrust the tickets at the scalper's chest, but the shorter man just let them fall to the ground.

Then the little crook's face twisted into an angry glare. He commenced with a stream of outrage that not even Ricky could comprehend. His arms began to thrust and turn in rhythm with his rant. White spittle pooled at the outer edges of his mouth. It was the most aggressive verbal assault I had ever seen in my life. The German's companion pulled at his collar from behind. He was still angry but suddenly apprehensive. The assailed scalper was now unassailable.

The German took a step backward and the scalper took a step forward. The stout Italian crept forward, all the while continuing his irate tantrum. The little crook lifted his hands in front of his chest, shouted something and thrust his arms forward with a push. He wasn't close enough to make contact with the German, but he didn't need to be. The German flinched backward, tripped, and caught himself on the sturdy chain running along the edge of the jetty. If not for that chain, he would have been in the harbor.

The German man grabbed his lady by the hand and retreated. He looked back several times as he hurried down the jetty. His face twisted with frustration and disbelief. The little crook picked the tickets up off the ground and scurried down a dark passage running along the far side of the castle.

"He looked like a pissed off pit bull tugging at his leash," I said as the crowd of patrons murmured around us. The buzz was invigorating.

We laughed at the absurdity, then Ricky asked me, "You know why dogs bark at mailmen?"

"No, tell me."

"It makes them feel dominant. They bark, the mailman leaves. Every day this happens."

"So?"

"The dog thinks he's dominant because his aggression is always rewarded."

I set my beer down and leaned into Ricky. "Are you one of those sophisticated motherfuckers?"

He ignored me. "The dog's like, yeah, that's right, get off my porch, I'm the alpha here."

"A point, does this story have one?"

"There are lots of assholes running these streets every night." Ricky pointed back towards shore. Far off, a scooter ascended a dark, narrow street into the Spanish Quarter of Naples, a neighborhood where all the locals cautioned us not to tread. "First they rip you off, and if you stick up for yourself, then they bark in your face."

"What do you care?" I placed my left palm atop the gift box once more.

"It pisses me off. Nothing pisses me off more than a bully."

"They're ripping off tourists; happens every day in every city."

Ricky lifted his beer and pointed it toward me. "It's like you said, then. The whole world is one city."

"Cheers."

"Cheers."

I never thought you could make something as simple as pizza so outstanding until I went to Napoli. Being from Chicago, Ricky was less generous with his praise, but even he said it was great.

"Like this," Ricky instructed as he tapped the edge of his plate with his knife to get my attention.

Tink Tink

Rick put the tip of his knife in the very middle of the pizza and cut toward the crust. Using both his fork and knife, he rolled the mini slice inwards from the middle to make a pinwheel pastry of the pizza. He popped the little roll in his mouth, savored it and swallowed. "You get all the different flavors of the dough and the cheese this way. The undercooked parts towards the center are soft and subtle, while the charred parts of the crust have a toasted nut flavor."

I followed suit. "Tastes like pizza."

After dinner, Ricky ordered coffee for both of us. The waiter brought out a little pot for us to share. It was like the small percolator my dad used to bring when we went camping. After we spilled out all the coffee, I picked it up and examined it. For the life of me, I couldn't figure out where they put the coffee in, much less how it worked.

Ricky took the machine from my hands. "It's called a Mokka." He grabbed the top with one hand and placed the bottom in his other palm. He twisted with a grunt and it unscrewed into two pieces. He placed the top to the side and then extracted the metal filter from the bottom reservoir."

"Ah ha." I pointed at the grounds that were hardened like a cake within the puck shaped filter. I brought the filter to my nose. "Mmm, smells good."

"Simple is superior."

I grabbed the reservoir and looked inside. "So, this is where you put the water?"

"Obviously . . ."

"What's the little line in there for?" There was a line etched in the inner wall of the reservoir about four fifths of the way up.

"That's the limit. You shouldn't go past that line."

I nodded and looked off towards the Spanish Quarter.

Ricky and I split up after dinner. He headed back to meet his band. We had grown close during the tour, and I was really looking forward to hooking up with him again back in the States, but that never happened. He fell in with another group called the Polyglots. They scored a big hit when they did a punk cover of a Nora Lynn Donovan song. Something from her dark period, after she overdosed.

I headed to the Spanish Quarter and walked until I found "Spaccanapoli" street. Ricky had told me that Spaccanapoli means "splits Naples," and that it's the Main Street of the city. It looked nothing like the Main Street of any town I had ever seen. It was dark, dirty, and forbidding, even more so than the rest of the city. The streets were made of large black lava stones. The street was pitched outward from the center to allow liquids and filth to roll into stone gutters on each side. Above the gutters were storefronts and other businesses. Almost everything was shuttered, except for the restaurants and vendors selling food and drink from storefront windows.

The buzz-saw exhaust of a scooter roared behind me. There were two men in the seat and the one on the back had a satchel slung over his shoulder. I saw wine bottle tops protruding from the bag. They slowed down to make a turn and the man on the back looked back at me. He wore a red bandana over his face like a bandit.

The street was so narrow I couldn't believe it was permissible for traffic. As though anyone gave a shit about permission in this place, I suppose. The narrow canyon walls of the street widened somewhat further up the block. As I got closer, I noticed a church on the left. It had a small swath of concrete in front of the steps. Scooters were parked side by side all along the front as though the church was some type of biker bar for midgets. Iron railings extended up each side of the steps and the newel posts at the bottom were topped with balusters in the form of iron skull sculptures. The crowns of the skull tops were polished clean and bright after years of passersby rubbing the tops. A brown sign explained the significance of the church, but I didn't bother to read it. As I turned to leave I noticed a rival church across the street. It also had a brown sign. The two churches faced each other like boxers in the middle of a ring, one determined to dominate the other.

I walked another block down and saw a souvenir store that had a rosary like the one I carried in the box under my arm. As I peered in the showcase window to catch a price, the proprietor shut the steel shutter right before my eyes.

Clang

Just one beat after that, the herd of scooters parked near the church roared to life. The riders were mounted two to a saddle and headed down the same alley the first pair had gone. The buzzing whine of their motors faded long after the last riders disappeared. I was left in a lonely silence in a place where neither silence nor loneliness was the norm.

I walked back to the opposing churches. It no longer felt like they were trying to dominate each other. It felt like they were both peering down at me with shrugged shoulders, saying I don't know, bud, feels like you could be missing something.

I don't wear a watch. You would think as a drummer I would be more concerned about time, but I just never saw the point of a watch. If everyone else has a watch, why do I need to buy one? In any case, I guessed that it must be close to 9:00 pm at this point, since that's what time everyone said they were meeting back at Corso Garibaldi and everyone seemed to have disappeared from Spaccanapoli.

I walked the corridor all the scooters had gone down. There was an arched portico at the end of the way. Beyond the portico was a main traffic artery of the city, and it was choked with people marching and shouting. I jumped in the flow and floated amongst the people. It had the same energy as a mosh pit except no one was trying to boot me in the ass or elbow me in the ear. They were aggressive, to be sure, but their angst was directed at a very specific individual: George W. Bush.

All kinds of Bush effigies bobbed down the street. There was a gallery's worth of animated signs, with Bush guzzling oil or burning babies or acting as a puppeteer for his regime of willing allies. And one really vulgar poster had Bush chugging a beer as he rammed Berlusconi in the ass.

There was a din of random chants, though sometimes the crowd pulled together for a decent chorus or two. One thing they were shouting sounded like Ass ass eeno. I liked that one, so I joined in.

In retrospect, I know I heard the tear gas guns pop off, but I gave it no regard at the time. It wasn't until I saw the fluffy clouds of thick smoke that I put two and two together. It seemed so premature. We weren't really doing anything but marching up the street and yelling a bunch of gibberish. I remember thinking to myself that if the cops wanted to escalate things, this was the perfect way to do it.

As it turns out, we were being corralled. As we drew closer to the end of the block we saw another set of protesters another block down, faced off against another group of cops, who probably felt they were about to be crushed between the two groups of protesters. They had sent tear gas into the front of that crowd as well. Our crowd took a right at the end of the block. The other crowd took a left and I had no idea where any of us were headed, so I stopped at one of the little bodegas and bought myself a beer.

The cashier popped the top of my Peroni. I walked outside and leaned against the wall. I watched the people march by. There were mostly young, smiling faces. They had zeal, and they were passionate in their opposition to the war, but more than anything they really seemed to be enjoying themselves. Not everyone had signs and not everyone was chanting. Lots of folks looked like they were just along for the ride. I spied a young couple strolling hand in hand as the crowd grew thinner toward the end. After the tail of the procession passed, a team of cops followed at a safe distance. I went into the store and bought another beer.

I came back out and followed the mounted police at a safe distance as well. The street was a mess of litter, bottles and horse shit. As I navigated the piles, I looked up at the light standards lining the block and noticed their ornamentation for the first time. The black iron poles were sculpted like tied bundles of thin sticks that gave way to a bouquet of leaves at the top. Emerging from the bouquet was a woman, topless, holding the light fixture in her raised arms. This city was as beautiful as it was dirty.

As I continued up the street, I saw that the mounted police were stopped in the street, barricaded by a pile of burning garbage and scrap wood. The rear guard of the mob was prepared. They clearly had a strategy, and I was impressed.

A waft of black smoke hit one of the horses in the face. She whinnied and sneezed as she turned away. She bumped the horse to her right and that horse got pissed. She reared and soon all eight of the horses were stomping and bucking in disapproval of the whole situation.

One cop pulled the reins hard to the right and the horse turned completely around. The cop saw me and glared. I raised my arms with the gift box in one hand and a bottle of beer in my hand as if to say, *No worries, just enjoying the show.*

He understood things differently. What he saw was a punk kid with a suspicious package and a bottle ready to launch at him. I froze, frowned and broke down the closest alley I could find. I gambled that the guy wouldn't break ranks from the others and, thankfully, I was right.

The alley let out to a large square. People gathered there but it was a different vibe. Their focus was an stone spike at the center of the square. The length of the object was decorated with angels and other religious stuff. There was a cross at the top. Instead of carrying signs, these people carried candles. Instead of protest chants, these people were praying. This city was as friendly as it was dangerous.

Shouts and a commotion came from one corner of the square, disturbing the serenity of the moment. All heads turned to see a band of people sprint into the square with wild eyes and mouths covered by bandanas, rags, or their own shirts. First ten, then thirty, then fifty people flooded in, followed by a team of cops with their bastions unsheathed. Their masks were down, and the lights of the square shimmered on their heavy plastic shoulder pads. There were only about twenty of these riot police, but they were followed by two armored personnel carriers. The armored vehicles were equipped with four water cannons each.

The newcomers crowded around and then mixed with the prayer group. Some of the religious folks pulled the masked bandits within their group to shield them from the impending punishment. There was a brief stalemate. The cops stopped in perfect formation as the crowd murmured before them. I felt my breath heaving in my chest. I was exhaling out my nose like a furious bull. I clutched my package so hard that my fingertips began to tear the paper.

I was scared but vested at this point. I negotiated my opposing impulses. The dominant thought was to bolt for the opposite corner of the square and get the hell out of there, but following very close behind was the urge to stick around and watch the pandemonium that was about to ensue. I eyed a storefront on my side of the square that was still lit. It looked like a safe spot and they might even have beer, I thought.

I approached the storefront and not only was it open, it was teeming with action. It wasn't a store at all, but a social club. Jackpot.

Old men smoked and played cards. A barman served cocktails at one end and a barista served coffee at the other. Men shot billiards in the back while others played the video poker machines lining the left wall. The clientele was oblivious to the chaos about to erupt outside.

I took a confident stride into the place like a cowboy heading through the swinging doors of a saloon. I made it two more strides and was halted by two large men dressed in black. They stood in front of me. They were taller than me by a full head.

"Ferma," the one on the left said and raised his palm toward me. He shook his head no and smiled.

"Fuori," the other said and pointed to the door. He gave me the same smile.

I understood their Italian perfectly. I pouted a little and they shrugged in response. I pointed to the bar and mimed my desire for just one beer. They shook their heads no. I turned and walked out the door.

The bandits were now arm in arm with the holy rollers in the square. They faced the police and sang church hymns, or so it sounded to me. This was a letdown. I strolled to the opposite corner of the square to make my way back to the train station. As I turned in that direction, I heard loud shouts and breaking glass coming from around the corner.

Another gang of masked youths erupted into the square in a wild panic. One kid held a green bottle with a flaming rag hanging out of the top. He juked left and right as a cop tailed him with a club, swinging for his head. The kid tossed the bottle backward over his head with no care as to where it went or what it hit. It broke on the ground and the liquid inside splashed into flames that spread across the concrete. Everyone just ran straight through the flames. Cops poured into the square like sheets of rain.

The cops in the opposite corner of the square seized the occasion to advance on the makeshift choir. In full armor, with masks down, shields forward and clubs out, they tightened around the mass of people. Then they beat the ever-loving shit out of them with glee.

I stood still with my back against the wall, outside of their perimeter. I clutched my mother's gift with both hands. My legs trembled. I was poised to bolt left or right should any threat come my way. My chest ballooned with each breath and my vision was acute. Time slowed.

I watched as a cop walloped the legs of a kid with his baton. He moved up and down from ankles to thighs and peppered his knees for good measure. The boy covered his head with both arms and absorbed each blow with a scream.

All the candles were extinguished by now. People climbed the pedestal of the obelisk and a few had managed to scale the pillar itself. A waifish girl wrapped her arms around the neck of a cherub angel and swung. Cops pulled her down with no care for how she landed on the cobblestones below.

I saw one boy swing a two-by-four round and round in a ferocious spasm. He was seized by three cops but not before he managed to knock the baton from one cop's hand. The club flew toward me and landed with a rattle just ten feet away. A young bandit came and grabbed it. He returned to the scrum and jumped into the air. He held the club high above his head at his apex and brought it down with a thundering crash on the mask of a cop.

Crack

"This is some real hoodlum shit," I said out loud to no one.

The cops had advanced too far. They were too concentrated in the center. Their ranks were broken and the rioters were now mixed in with them. The prayer group folks were now just as violent as anyone else. The tide swung and the mob gained the advantage.

Now the rioters were more vicious than the cops. They lacked all self-control. One member of the gang found a loose cobblestone, pried it out and pitched it square in the back of one of the cops. He pulled another of the black lava stones from the ground and passed it to a nearby rioter. He pulled another, then another, then another, as fast as he could. He passed them around and soon the rocks rained down on the cops like magma from Vesuvius. The cops lost all will, and when the tables were turned, they cowered. Some ran, surrendering their shields and batons as they scurried to the safety of the armored vehicles. I had never been so entertained in my life.

Once enough cops had retreated, I heard a whistle and then a chorus of whistles. Holy shit, is there someone reffing all this? I thought. How could this get any more insane?

At the sound of the whistle, all the remaining cops in the square retreated to the armored carriers. The carriers advanced

with the cops walking behind them. The water cannons commenced to power wash the square, scouring the surface of
everyone and everything. The loose cobblestones skipped along
the ground like rubber balls. Clothing was ripped clean off anyone the cannons made contact with.

The crowd lost their resolve. The advancing cannons pushed
the crowd from the center to a corner of the square. It was impossible to see through the splashing and the mist of the water
jets shooting across the ground. The cops flanked out to the left
and right of the carriers. I imagined that they were going to con-
verge and squeeze the protesters out of the square like a zit.

Then a cannon was pointed at me. I ran toward the same corner of the square the rioters were headed. With my back turned,
I was rammed with a blast of water. The package flew from my
hands and skipped along the ground. I jumped forward to grab
it, but it was kicked ahead by someone running from the cannons. I found it and ran toward it, but I was hit with another
blast of water and propelled to the ground.

I remember that the blast hurt. It hurt even more to smack
the ground, but the real shock came from the cold. The freezing
water made me gasp for air and then the cold clung to me from
head to toe. I shook off some water and rose to my knees. I
looked around for my package. It had been kicked to the curb
and was floating in the gutter. I ran and retrieved it.

The bow was undone and the paper wrapping was soaked
and worthless, so I tore all the covering off. What was left was
a sturdy white box, still intact. I sprinted forward into the crowd
carrying the box like a running back carrying a football. I bull-
dozed through people like I was headed downfield for a
touchdown. It was pandemonium. I couldn't care less about
who I trampled.

I ran and ran until my lungs burned and my gut ached. I made
turns in whichever direction the crowd was not going. When I
finally felt alone and secure, I slowed down. I knelt over and
began to cough. I almost puked, too, but I choked it back. I

finally caught my breath and when I looked up, I saw the giant portrait of Castro and Che up the street on the left. I looked at all the shops lining the right side of the street. Any of those without a steel gate had their windows busted out and were looted. I saw a bakery with a massive void where a picture window had been. A large, multi-tiered cake was featured on a pedestal. Someone had jammed their hand in the base and scooped out a large hunk of it.

Many of the places with the protective steel gate were smoking from the inside. The gates on others must have been weak or just for show because they were ripped out and the places looked combed through. I walked up the street looking for the Idraulico sign and the little shop where I bought the rosary. I prayed the place was intact and that Angelo and Lucia were ok.

I found the Idraulico—the plumber, that is—the place was fine. I traced my steps to the gift shop, where I found the steel gate twisted and crumpled like scrap paper on the ground. The door was busted, and the windows were broken.

I walked in the shop and saw Angelo and Lucia behind the counter. Angelo held a bloody bandage around his hand. Lucia held one to her head. They stared at me, stoic and silent. I doubt they recognized me. *Do your worst, we have nothing left to lose*, their faces said.

"I'm so sorry." I held the package in my hand. I held it up slightly to remind them who I was and that I meant them no harm. "Thanks again for this."

They just stared at me. I looked around the shop. All the coins were gone, as was the silverware. The delicate glass shades of the lamps that had lined the walls were now shattered on the floor. Some of the war medals were still there but all the sunglasses were gone. I scanned the store until I reached the showcase where the rosary was and . . . there it was. The rosary, my rosary, was displayed just as before in the same place Ricky and I had first found it.

I looked down at my gift box. Lucia stood up and walked to the back of the shop. I opened the top of the box and looked inside. I removed a piece of tissue paper, and then another, and then another. Then I saw it: a length of thick, red yarn coiled in the box. The yarn was bright, fire red, just like the rosary. If I had spied her putting it in the box from a distance, I would have thought it was the rosary itself.

Rage percolated inside me and then boiled over. I crumpled the box in my hands. I grabbed the base of a lamp from the floor. I smashed and cleared what was left of the glass of the showcase that held my rosary. I reached in and seized it. Then I went to the showcase with the medals and I took the Purple Heart.

I looked at Angelo. He stared straight ahead.

I imagined how they must have laughed after I, another sucker, left their store. I imagined all the people they had ripped off and all the people who had their treasures stolen to fill the shelves. I spun into a frenzy of hate and began to pull the show-cases down to the ground one after another. I was a one-man mosh pit of demolition. I pulled the maps and banners off the walls, ripping them as best I could and then stomping on them. I wanted to finish the job the looters hadn't finished. If I had had a flamethrower, I would have used it.

When I was done, I looked straight at Angelo and spit on the floor.

Glass crackled beneath my feet as I turned to walk out the door.

Crunch

I noticed a wristwatch amongst the destruction. I retrieved it, shook it off, and put it on. It was time for me to catch the next train to Rome.

6

NOBODY KNOWS NORA

Nora sat in the studio of the home she had bought for her parents. Not only had she bought the home, she had helped design it, inside and out. It was a handsome Georgian with five bedrooms and six bathrooms. The house was more than she ever dreamed she could have for herself, much less gift away before she turned twenty-five.

When she presented the house to her parents they were delighted that she had chosen to buy a home so close to theirs. Her father, Roger, assessed the fireplaces. Her mother, Claudia, ran her finger along the walnut chair rail.

"Are you planning on having friends over when you're in town, Lenora?" Claudia asked.

Nora giggled, "Probably, now that you mention it." Then she laughed a little more before covering her mouth with her hand. She was enjoying the slow deal.

"This is going to take a lot to keep clean," Roger said. Nora expected this from her dad. She knew how proud he was of her; she didn't need gasps and gushing from him. She knew he would be looking out for the downside, reminding her of the responsibilities that come with success.

"Well, I was thinking you and Mom would handle that," Nora said and giggled again.

Roger scoffed. Claudia looked at her husband, screwed her face tight and turned to Nora. "I think we've done more than our part, young lady."

Nora giggled again.

Roger and Claudia looked at each other, puzzled. Roger asked, "What are you on?"

Nora composed herself. She pulled a stool up to the marble island in the middle of the kitchen. "I'm not on anything, Daddy. I'm just happy. This is a big day for me."

"Well, do tell. This must be something very big," Roger said. "It's not like this is the first place you've ever bought."

"It's the first place I've ever bought for my parents, though." Nora's smile stretched far across her face.

The expression on Roger's face warped from surprise to happiness and then to concern. He shook his head no. "Our house is perfectly fine. That's where you were raised."

Nora looked at her father and nodded. He just said exactly what she expected him to say. Claudia said nothing for the moment. She smiled and pulled a stool next to Nora at the island. She placed her right hand on top of her daughter's left.

"Congratulations, Lenora. I'm so proud of you." Claudia leaned over and hugged her daughter around the shoulders. Nora shrunk into her mother's embrace. "I know what this means. I get it."

With that, Roger relaxed. He looked up and noticed the coffered ceilings for the first time. He put his hands in his pockets and began to stroll around the floor. He followed the crown molding tracing the ceiling and let it lead him from room to room.

The basement area was actually a 2,000-square-foot apartment with a bedroom, two bathrooms, bar, full kitchen and two separate entrances. The foundation was dug deep, so the apartment had twelve-foot ceilings. There was a fireplace. Most importantly, there was a simple music studio.

The recording floor had a drum kit, a few guitars, a keyboard and a vocals "closet" where the singer could cordon herself off from the instruments. Her style of music required nothing more. On the other side of the glass was just enough space for the technical equipment and a creative desk in the control room. The recording floor and the control room were dark, save for a lamp that cast its light over the pad of paper on which Nora wrote.

. . . you're always saying thank you when I come home like I'm doing you some favor. Don't you understand that I need you? I need you more than you need me. Everywhere I go now, everyone I see—even old friends—people act like they are being received by the Pope. I don't need that. I don't want that. But there's no end in sight.

There was a rap on the door. Claudia's moon face peered through the diamond-shaped, double-paned window of the door. Nora covered her pad with her arm and waved her in.

"Are you writing, sweetie?" Claudia asked.

"No, it's origami. New hobby." She pointed at the pad of paper. "I call this one Surface of Pond on a Quiet Summer Morning."

"Don't be a smart aleck."

"Yes, I'm writing. What's up?"

"You're cousins are coming for dinner."

"Which cousins?"

"The Phelans."

"The who?"

"The Phelans, my cousin's kids," Claudia offered. "Bobby, Billy, Brenda, Becky and Bethany."

"Ah, the killer Bs. Are they bringing friends?"

"Well, Becky is married now, and the others may bring guests, I suppose." Claudia saw how this news weighed on Nora. "They're our family, honey. These aren't fan-club people."

"So many though?"

"I'm sorry, but we're Irish. That's how it goes." Claudia shrugged.

Nora affected her best Irish brogue, "Aye, doncha tink Mister Phelan could leave da missus to her stories fer joost woon night?"

Mother and daughter laughed together.

"Get back to your writing. They won't be here until suppertime, so you have plenty of time to relax," Claudia told her.

Nora returned to her letter.

Dr. Close says it's normal to feel lonely in my position but I don't understand how I can feel so empty with so many people around. I don't feel whole. I am a shell and these people only want to take a picture with the shell and say they met the shell. And another thing: I hate it when they use my full name. These "friends" of mine, I can hear them talking to their friends, probably their real friends, and I hear when they call me "Nora Lynn Donovan." Friends don't call

*each other by their full names. It should be "Noree" or "Ra Ra" like
Jen used to call me. I miss Jen.*

*I keep them around because I have to. John says a constant coterie
signals significance and once you have significance, you need to hold
on as hard as you can. He's a good manager. He got me this far. I
guess I should listen to him, but I still feel empty. I know it sounds odd,
but I feel even lonelier with a lot of people around.*

Nora looked up from her letter at the menagerie of awards
lining the floating shelves above the desk. The walls were fes-
tooned with posters promoting tours past, photographs from
concerts and pictures of her with the various celebrities she had
met. She looked at pictures taken from when she was a teenager,
when she first broke out. She frowned. At twenty-seven years
old, she felt old.

Her gaze returned to the top shelf above the desk, to her
award for Best New Artist. She could see the tarnish building on
its surface. Nora felt for the knob of the top drawer of the desk.
She opened it and retrieved a bottle of pills. She peered at the
label.

Oxycontin

She extracted one pill. It was round, corn-flower blue with an
indentation delineating the diameter. She used her thumb nail to
chop the pill in half along the line and placed the other half back
in the bottle. She pooled up some saliva in her mouth and
popped the half-pill in and then swallowed.

*I just want the pain to go away. I want the darkness to go away. I've
tried. I've tried so hard. I've gone to the therapist. I took the meds. I've
done everything I was told. I just want to feel better. I can't exist like
this any longer. I'm sorry, I love all of you so much, but this sadness . .*

. if you could just feel this sadness for a minute, you would understand. And I know you love me, and I know that should be all I need, and it makes me feel even worse that it's not. But if your love isn't enough to get me through, what possibly could?

It's not because James left, so don't go blaming him. My moods drove him away. And we were too young. It's ridiculous to think it would have worked. I don't want to write anything else about that, just don't blame him, ok?

Please believe me when I tell you that I tried. I know I'm repeating myself, but I did everything you told me. I see Dr. Close every week. Even when I'm touring we'll have calls. I take the meds, I quit drinking (as much), I run every morning, I pray, I find time for charity, I find time for family. I'd say I find time for friends, but I'm not sure who those are anymore.

I think about quitting and coming home but then what am I left with? Who am I? What am I? What do I do with my life? I've been training for this or doing this my whole life. When I get up tomorrow, where do I go, who do I call?

I feel like I'm a fraud to you and I'm sorry. I put on this happy face and joke around because it's easier for you. I don't want to scare you like I did after James left. I'm sorry for that, too, but you know that. The truth is, I haven't gotten better. I've gotten worse and there's nothing left to do.

Tears welled in her eyes and swelled until they yielded to gravity. She placed her palms on the desk and her face above the notepad. She watched the tears pool in her eyes and then drop to the pad. As each drop fell there was a moment of clarity before the next tears pooled. She could see that the tears were smearing the ink, but she did not care. She was satisfied with the effect; it added weight to her testament. She was an artist, after all.

Nora did not wail or sob or make any other noise as she cried. This was normal by now. The tears were proof she could still experience sadness, but she was numb to the actual act of crying. It just happened. Indeed, sadness was the only emotion that happened. She never got angry anymore, or excited, or afraid. She was aware of those feelings inside of her, but they passed through her like watching a burglar pillage your home as you sit and watch. Take what you need, just leave me be was what ran through her head most of the time.

She woke when her head hit the desk. She looked at her watch and made a note in the margin of the pad: *2:15, 22 minutes for ½ Ox.*

She returned to her letter. She read it again from the beginning. She picked up her pen.

I have no regrets. It sounds ridiculous, but I have no regrets. I'm just supposed to feel this way and it just needs to end this way. Look at my life. If someone can't be happy with all I have done in 27 years, they're simply not capable of happiness. And that's OK. I did a lot in 27 years. I am proud of the things I accomplished. And of course, I owe all of that to you two.
I guess I do have one regret. I regret what this is going to do to you two. But please believe me, this is a ~~release~~ relief. This is the most relieved I've felt since I can remember. I'm calm. I have no fear. This is how things are supposed to be.

Nora reached into the drawer and found the bottle of pills. She spilled out a bunch on top of the notepad. She did some quick math in her head and then counted out six. She placed the rest back in the bottle and placed the bottle back in the drawer. She was careful not to take too many. If she vomited them up after she passed out, she wouldn't die.

She held the pills in her left fist. She realized she would need something to wash them down this time. She left the studio and walked toward her basement kitchen, still clutching her pills.

Her father came down the stairs. "Hey there, sunshine," he said.

Nora froze. She eyed the half empty bottle of cabernet on the countertop. "Hey, Daddy."

"I thought I'd come hang out down here before the company comes. Is that OK?"

Nora subconsciously slammed her tear ducts shut, screamed an internal scream and reset her mood. She smiled. "I'd like that, Daddy."

Roger opened the fridge and grabbed a beer. Nora slipped open a drawer and let the pills fall from her hand. Roger turned and cracked open his beer.

"Happy hour?" Nora smiled again.

"It's always happy hour for me when you're home." He stroked his thumb down Nora's cheek. His thumb tracked the course of tears that had fallen earlier.

Nora grabbed a glass from the rack and then swiped the bottle of wine from the counter. She gripped the protruding cork in her teeth and pulled it out with a yank of her head. She turned her head and spit the cork towards the garbage can.

Puh-TEW

The cork rimmed and rattled before falling to the bottom.

"Classy," her father said. They walked to the couches in the basement living room.

"That was, like, eight feet. Give me some credit." Nora pointed at the bin. She set the empty glass and open bottle on the end table and then sat on the couch. She pulled her legs beneath her and then a knit blanket across her lap. Her father sat on the loveseat.

"I thought wine drinkers were supposed to be more sophisticated?"

"They say you reach your peak level of sophistication at age seventeen. Everything after that is an act," she answered. "For girls that is, boys are much later."

"Who's 'they'?"

"Dr. Close."

Roger sipped his beer. For a moment, the conversation stopped. The silence was out of rhythm from the banter leading up to that point. He swallowed his beer.

"How's that going?" he asked as if they were talking about a candle-making class.

"Very therapeutic," she said and then grinned.

Her father stared down the chamber of his beer can and laughed a little. He reached for the bottle of wine and drew her glass closer.

"You can't let me drink alone," he said and tried to pour.

Nora reached out and grabbed the bottle by the neck. She placed it back down on the table.

"You have to let me," Nora told him.

"Let you what?"

"You have to let me pour my own glass."

He sat back and nodded. "I guess I'm not familiar with the etiquette."

Nora poured the claret wine into her goblet. "It's just something I have to do for myself."

"Ah yes, my independent girl. I could never get you to listen to me, much less pour you a glass of wine," Roger said with pride, not frustration. "Here's to your homecoming honey. I love you."

"I love you too, Daddy."

He raised his beer can and Nora extended her glass towards him.

Clink

Roger took a swig of beer. Nora brought the rim of the glass to her mouth and let the liquid touch her lips. She set the glass down and wiped her lips with her index finger.

"How long are you staying?" he asked.

"I have a New Year's Eve show in Austin," she answered.

He was delighted. "Home for Thanksgiving and Christmas?"

"Unless something pulls me away," Nora said. Her mouth formed into a straight line and her round cheeks puffed out. It was a childish expression that he knew very well.

"You never know where you will end up tomorrow, do you?" he said. "You keep me young, sweetie. Without you, we would be leading very boring lives."

"What's that like?" Nora asked. "Boredom?"

Nora had never experienced boredom, she had never known ennui. Even before the fame struck, she was in training for fame: theatre, music, dance, and gymnastics. She missed all the parties and school dances. The things she skipped were the things other kids did to escape their boredom.

"Boredom is like . . ." Roger started. "It's like . . . when it's Saturday night and no one is doing anything and there's nothing on TV and you don't feel like doing anything but it's too early for bed and you're not tired anyway."

Nora puckered her lips and scrunched her mouth to the right. Another childish expression that told her father she didn't understand.

He tried again. "It's like when you're just existing. Like, you're alive but you have nothing to do and no reason to be." He realized he sounded pretty grim. "Don't get me wrong," he corrected himself. "We all have a reason to be. I just mean that, sometimes, we forget and that's when boredom happens."

"No, I get it. I get it." Nora said. "Does it ever, like, not go away?"

"Not go away, how?"

"Like, do you ever have a hard time escaping that feeling? That feeling that you have no reason to be?"

"I dunno. I suppose sometimes it's harder to shake off, but then, like I said, you keep us young."

Nora nodded. "How about when you were younger? Before I came around?"

"Oh sure, I remember being a teenager with nothing to do, after I got my license and before I discovered this stuff." He shook his can like a rattle. The foam rushed to the top of the can and he slurped it with his mouth.

"Me and my buddies, Don and Eddie, we'd drive out south to the lakes and get lost."

"Get lost?"

"Yeah, we'd try to get lost. We'd find the wooded roads and just drive and drive, making random turns along the way. We'd kill the lights anytime we saw a street sign." He blinked and reflected for a moment.

"So, did you do it? Did you get lost?" Nora sat forward.

"We sure did." Roger smiled. "One time we didn't make it home until two in the morning."

"Weren't Grandma and Grandpa mad?"

"Oh my, yes, they were livid." He stared ahead and thought to himself some more. "Don was driving, and he panicked. He needed to have the car back by midnight and we knew we were at least a half hour from home. He picked a direction and insisted we were going the right way. He had us going south and he just wouldn't listen when we told him there wasn't twenty miles of farmland between the lakes and home."

Nora watched her father as he smiled and reflected.

"That doesn't sound very boring," she said.

"It wasn't. It wasn't at all." He snapped out of it. "Sorry, yes, we were saying . . . have I ever been bored, for a long time, that was the question, right?"

"I'm jealous of you."

"You're jealous of ME?"

"I would trade a world tour to get lost with some old friends right now."

Roger inched closer to her. He clasped his beer in both hands and his elbows were on his knees. "Do you want to go for a drive with me right now? I'm not sure we can get lost before dinner, but we can try."

"I'm going to sleep now, Daddy." Nora reached out and touched his cheek.

"OK, sounds good." He stood and finished his beer. He reached to retrieve Nora's wine glass but noticed it was still full. "Do you want me to come down to wake you?"

"No, thank you." She looked away from him. "Maybe send one of the cousins down, when they get here."

Roger took the first few stairs and stopped. He turned and faced his daughter. "I love you," he said.

"I love you too, Daddy," Nora said.

Her father continued up the stairs. Once she heard the door close, Nora went to the kitchen and opened the drawer where she had stashed the pills. She plucked them out one by one. She counted them in her open palm and once she was sure she had all six, she put them in her mouth. Then she washed them down with her glass of wine.

James is driving. He's driving so fast. I tell him to slow down but he can't hear me. I yell but he still can't hear me. He has both hands on the wheel. He is gritting his teeth and staring straight ahead. There is a dream catcher hanging from the mirror. Its woven center is torn.

The highway is wide. We turn right into a curve and the car drifts left from the ass end. I expect us to hit a middle rail but there is none, there are just more and more lanes to the left. Our direction is more lateral than forward. We are driving into on-coming traffic. Cars whiz past us with their horns blaring. Then the rear tires gain purchase and we bolt back across the highway. A car scrapes our side and sparks fly.

We are on the right side of the highway now but James drives straight across those lanes too. We drive across the shoulder and over the edge of the highway. There is a steep slope and we have shot over it. We are airborne. All I see is blue sky across the windshield until the front end dips enough for me to see the ap-proaching ground. We fall slower now. The car follows a perfect tangent to the slope of the embankment and we touch down seamlessly. The car rolls forward down the hill and we slide to a halt.

James shuts off the car. He reaches in the center console and hands me a gumball. I put it in my mouth and chew. My teeth shatter. I place the intact gumball in the fore of my mouth, purse my lips and spit it out.

Puh-TEW

The gumball smacks the windshield.

PING

It rolls along the dashboard and I see that it's not a gumball but a large, tiger's eye marble. The swirled pattern inside the orb is orange and black.

The broken pieces of my teeth feel like shards of glass in my mouth. I rake my tongue with my fingers to remove the broken pieces of teeth. Some shards have fallen to my throat and I wretch to dislodge them. I hack a tooth-flecked film of blood and saliva onto the floor mat.

I sit up and open the vanity mirror to inspect the damage. My teeth are intact. They are bright and straight, and my mouth is clean. As I sit back in my seat, I notice something in the background of the mirror. It is a streetscape of derelict stores. I look closer and now I am standing on that street.

Now I am running down that street. There is a crowd around me. I am in a race. I veer to the edge of the course to take a cup of water. There is a line of women on the sidewalk holding paper cups. Each time I reach for a cup, they pull it away and then throw it at me. Each cup is full of confetti and glitter. The women have young faces, like children. They cheer as they pepper me with fanfare.

I am at the front of the pack now. I turn and I see only dogs. They are black and white shepherds. They nip and bite at my ankles and calves. I try to run faster but my legs will not propel me faster. I turn to kick at the dogs, but my leg moves in slow motion. Even when I do land a strike, it is weak and useless. I am surrounded by dogs for a moment but they part to make way towards a storefront. I face the store and the dogs behind begin to nip and bite at me again. I run into the store. The dogs bark and bellow with satisfaction.

The store is a church. It is my church. There is a coffin lying open and empty in front of the altar. I climb in and pull the top closed upon myself. It latches shut and I am in complete darkness. I am sealed tight in a cocoon of linen and silk lining. The cushioning of the casket walls hugs me. My entire body is held in the clutch of the box as the material conforms around my body. The cushion presses against my face and I feel the silk lining flutter against my cheeks as I exhale. I notice my breathing now.

I try to reach my hand to my face to clear space in front of my mouth, but my arms are stuck in position. I can barely breathe. I kick my legs to try to move upwards in hopes of finding more room, but I move nary an inch. I am suffocating in silk. I panic. I try to scream. I shake and contort my body, but I am squeezed tighter and tighter in the grip of my coffin.

Wake up. Wake up, Nora.

Oh, no. Oh, no, no, no.

Nora, you have to wake up.

I have to get out of here. Please get me out of here. I have to get out of here.

Please, Nora. Please.

Nora's eyes opened and she struggled to focus. Her father's arms were wrapped around her chest from the front. He was standing, holding up Nora's convulsing body from beneath her armpits. Claudia struggled to steady Nora's head as it swiveled to and fro like a heavy blossom on a weak stem. Nora wheezed and moaned. She struggled to say something but produced only grunts.

"Nora be quiet," her mother said as she cried.

Roger released a heavy, strained breath as he steadied his daughter's trembling torso.

Nora gained her footing and brought her back rigid. She heaved an unctuous slurry of bile and red wine down her chin and chest. She fell on her bottom and placed her palms on the floor. "I'm sorry, I'm so sorry."

Lenora carried a tray of champagne flutes as she strolled the floor of the gallery. She held the tray high and peered through the effervescent liquid at the crowd mingling within the event space. Three patrons were viewing a pop art piece by a local artist who was in the midst of transitioning in style and gender. One of the patrons signaled Lenora with a side glance, so she approached the woman. Two of the patrons were guests and the third was the transitioning artist.

"So what's your pronoun?" Lenora heard one of the guests ask the artist as she approached.

Lenora loved the job. It paid nearly nothing, but she had plenty of money anyway. She loved to catch snippets of conversation while also being completely ignored. She felt like a drone floating above the crowd, randomly engaging to drop a drink or morsel into their hands and then retreating to her orbit.

"Prosecco?" she asked as she approached the group of three.

"Is this champagne?" the artist asked.

"It's Prosecco," Lenora replied politely.

The guests and the artists each took a flute off the tray and returned to their conversation. Lenora turned and smiled. There were two glasses left on her tray.

A couple held hands as they walked the gallery. They moved quickly. They were still wearing their coats and scarves. Lenora guessed they had snuck in from their evening walk to see what all the fuss was about. She changed her orbit to intersect theirs.

"It's vengeance, but it's a vengeance that was born from a hundred mothers." The man said to his companion.

Before she could catch the woman's response, she heard a man scolding another man near one of the sculptures at the middle of the floor.

"If they don't give you credit, you have to take it," the authoritarian man said and pointed at the other man's chest, his finger only inches away. The other man nodded with a stern face. Lenora watched as the first man pointed with more and more vigor as the other man absorbed his message.

"Prosecco?" she offered the last two flutes but the pointing man waved her off.

The sculpture was a sad child holding a deflated balloon. The boy was bronze, but the balloon was real and on a nylon string. The boy stood atop a pedestal holding the string as the wilted balloon draped down the side. The title of the sculpture was It Gets Heavier As You Empty It.

There was music playing at a low volume. It was upbeat yet anodyne, as easily ignored as enjoyed.

Lenora floated to a small group near another painting. The artist was explaining the piece. "I was thinking of something so wonderful that it eventually overwhelms you, like diamonds or pretty women."

The painting was a solid blue stripe painted over a wider, yellow stripe.

There were no takers for her last two drinks. As she turned away from the group, two men also peeled away. The one spoke to the other with an English accent, "American or not, he's far from typical."

Then they grabbed the last two flutes from Lenora's tray without looking at her. She only noticed they were gone by the relief in weight from the tray. With all of her drinks gone, she headed to the staging area in the back.

Lenora found Jen. Jen was the owner of the catering company providing the service this evening.

"You make any new friends tonight, Ra Ra?" Jen asked her.

Lenora smiled. "Not yet but that's OK. You know I'm wary of anyone too eager to meet me."

Jen handed Lenora a tray of bacon-wrapped dates. Lenora hoisted it above her shoulder and grabbed a stack of napkins off the serving station.

Jen counseled her. "Well, sometimes you just need to listen. When people share it makes them vulnerable. But that means they trust you."

"Thanks, doc." Lenora plucked a treat from her tray and popped it in her mouth.

"You need to trust people sometimes, too. That's all I'm saying." Jen sent her on her way with a pat on the shoulder.

Lenora strutted her way back into the gallery. The tray of hors d'oeuvres was much easier to handle than the heavy tray of cocktails. On the downside, she had to push the food much harder than the alcohol.

The style of music changed at the top of the hour and the volume was turned up. Loud, retro pop music played, and Lenora recognized the tune.

"Oh my God. Is that Nora Lynn Donovan?" a woman said as she grabbed a date from the tray.

Lenora stared at the woman. Lenora reached out to hand the woman a napkin, but she didn't take it. "My name is Lenora," she told the stranger, who ignored her.

The woman cocked her head and held her right ear to the air. "Wow, I haven't heard this in years. Do you remember this?"

"I do." Lenora scanned the room looking for anyone who might want a date.

"I think she won one of those teeny bopper music competitions. That's what made her famous." The woman still had her ear cocked. She peered at the speaker as though some evidence in support of her point was forthcoming.

Lenora grabbed a date and popped it in her mouth. "Sounds about right," she said as she chewed.

"I hate when people turn art into competition. The arts are about collaboration. Don't you agree?" the woman asked.

Lenora swallowed. "Absolutely."

"Such a shame about Nora Lynn, though. Died so young." The woman shook her head.

Lenora's grip on the tray slipped. It drooped and the dates were poised to roll off onto the floor. "No, no, she's not dead."

"Well, her career sure is!" The woman laughed heartily and popped the date in her mouth.

Lenora forced a laugh and smiled. "I heard she's quite happy now."

The End

ABOUT THE AUTHOR

Otto Frank Miller is an author, statistician and financial professional. He is also an amateur musician whose only brush with fame was playing two measures of Hoochie Coochie Man at open mic night at Rosa's Lounge in Chicago before his amp lit on fire and he had to pitch it out the back door of the club. He is a lifelong Chicagoan save for several blurry years spent in Champaign, Illinois and another five lost in New York City. He now resides in Riverside, Illinois with his wife and daughters. Otto is a Scorpio.

www.ingramcontent.com/pod-product-compliance
Lightning Source LLC
Chambersburg PA
CBHW051959170626
46808CB00007B/2689